A HEART DIVIDED

During World War Two, the German occupation of Île d'Oleron, off the west coast of France, brings fear and hardship to the islanders. As the underground freedom-fighters strive to liberate their beloved island, Florentine Devreux finds her heart torn between two brothers. But it seems she has fallen in love with the wrong one! The events following the Normandy landings force her to think again — but has her change of heart come too late?

KAREN ABBOTT

A HEART DIVIDED

Complete and Unabridged

LINFORD
Leicester

First published in Great Britain in 2004

First Linford Edition
published 2005

British Library CIP Data

Abbott, Karen
    A heart divided.—Large print ed.—
Linford romance library
    1. Brothers—Fiction 2. World War, *1939 –
1945* —France—Fiction 3. Love stories
    4. Large type books
    I. Title
    823.9'14 [F]

ISBN 1–84395–897–X

Published by
F. A. Thorpe (Publishing)
Anstey, Leicestershire

Set by Words & Graphics Ltd.
Anstey, Leicestershire
Printed and bound in Great Britain by
T. J. International Ltd., Padstow, Cornwall

This book is printed on acid-free paper

1

When Corporal Florentine Devreux was summoned to appear before her commanding officer at the HQ behind the Allied lines, her mind ran swiftly over the previous twenty-four hours, wondering what sin she had committed to merit the summons.

She could think of nothing!

It was 1944 and the lives of millions of people had been turned upside down by the war that had swept across Europe and spilled over on to other continents. The war wasn't over yet . . . but a confidence was growing among the Allied armies that the end was in sight!

The depth of understanding in her commander's expression as she entered the room simultaneously both comforted and alarmed Florentine. It wasn't going to be a chastisement —

so what was it?

'You have been commended for a bravery-in-action medal, Corporal Devreux.' Commander Tranter smiled. 'For recognising the need for immediate action when the sergeant in charge of your platoon was unfortunately killed . . . and for deploying the rest of the platoon effectively whilst under fire. Your actions showed clarity of thinking under stressful conditions, coolness of mind and an ability to take command.'

Florentine reddened slightly, a few chestnut curls choosing that moment to spring from the confines of her regulation cap and dance around her face.

'The whole unit deserves the commendation, ma'am,' Florentine said quietly.

'Maybe so, but you were the one who took action and brought everything under control, in consequence of which, I now have the pleasure of promoting you to the rank of sergeant. Congratulations, Sergeant Devreux!'

Florentine dazedly took hold of her extended hand, her thoughts whirling. A commendation and her sergeant's stripes all in one day! Wow!

'Thirdly, Sergeant Devreux, I now offer you your honourable discharge from the army.'

Florentine's mind did a double take. Had she misheard? Honourable discharge? Surely not?

'Pardon, ma'am?'

Commander Tranter repeated her words, a flicker of amusement in her eyes as she took note of Florentine's confusion.

Florentine frowned.

'I . . . I don't understand, ma'am.'

'Stand easy, Sergeant Devreux.'

Florentine did so, still trying to make sense of the words her commanding officer had calmly spoken. Her eyes, the colour of dark honey, now sported bright highlights as the information so far given had penetrated into her agile brain. Something exciting was afoot.

'As you know, Sergeant, the allied armies have been moving forward through France after the successful landings in Normandy in June. Paris has been liberated . . . but the German army refuses to surrender.'

She paused and seemed to weigh her words before she continued in a softer tone. 'The powers-that-be have realised that a specific area of occupied France, Île d'Oleron, to be exact, must be liberated before we can consolidate our gain.'

Florentine listened with mounting excitement as Commander Tranter continued, her face taking on an added glow as she gradually began realising what its relevance was to her unexpected discharge from the army.

'My opposite number at HQ has gone through the files and has decided that you are the best person for the imminent undercover operation,' Commander Tranter continued. 'What I am about to tell you is strictly confidential and you are under stringent orders not to disclose a word of it to anyone. Is that clear?'

'Yes, ma'am,' she replied, her mind still reeling.

'Good. I will just run through your credentials to make sure no mistakes have been made. You are Florentine Devreux, born in 1923 on Île d'Oleron in the Charente Maritime region of south-western France?'

'Yes, ma'am.'

'You are a qualified radio technician and joined this regiment two years ago, since when you have been promoted to corporal, now sergeant, and have been on active service, sometimes under fire and have been commended for a bravery-in-action medal?'

She looked kindly at the dazed face of the young woman who stood before her and continued briskly, 'Your technical skills and the fact that Île d'Oleron is your home territory is the reason Intelligence has requested that you are seconded to the French unit. Once there, you will be fully briefed about your mission. All I can tell you is that you are to be put ashore on Île d'Oleron within the next few days. Since the landings, things are moving towards the big push, and, as you probably realise, Île d'Oleron holds a strong, strategic position.'

She looked up from the notes she was reading and added less formally, 'No doubt you are aware that the island has been under German occupation since early 1942?'

'Yes, ma'am, but I've not been back since just before that happened. I've had only two letters that the Resistance movement managed to smuggle out and they contained much censorship!'

She cast her mind back to her last few months on the island, now over three years ago. On the surface, life on the island had carried on as normal for the first year or so of the war, but youngsters like herself, too young to join the regular army, had formed secret resistance groups. Led by the more elderly ex-combatants from the

First World War, men who had thought never to be needed to use such skills again, they had learned the rudiments of guerrilla warfare.

Once the Germans had arrived, soon after her departure into the real army, she knew that many of those she left behind had continued with the work, now in earnest. How had they fared? Were they still active? Had any she knew been killed? Would any of her age group still be there?

Her heart skipped a beat as she thought of Pierre St Clare, three years older than her, a young man who had set many female hearts on fire, her own included. But he wouldn't be there! He'd be with the Allies on the mainland somewhere, making conquests wherever he went, no doubt. Married, perhaps? She hoped not! But, wherever he was, she hoped he was safe.

The voice of her commander broke into her thoughts. 'Papers are being prepared for you and a colleague, Corporal Barclay, who, I am given to understand, speaks excellent French.' She raised a questioning eyebrow.

'Yes, ma'am,' Florentine murmured in agreement again.

Someone had been very busy digging into her personal files. Was there anything they didn't know?

'You must understand that, as under-cover agents, you will be out of the protection of the Geneva Convention regulations concerning the fair treatment of prisoners of war,' Commander Tranter warned. 'Have you any questions to ask?'

Florentine was pleased to hear the name of her companion. They had enlisted at the same time and had been close friends from their early training days. As to the rest, her mind was spinning, full of questions, but none seemed appropriate to ask right then, knowing that times of departure, details of training required and other essentials would be given as needed.

'No, ma'am.'

'Good. I will be seeing Corporal

Barclay immediately after this interview. Return to barracks and pack your kit and then report back to me. The official line will be that you have been transferred to another battalion so keep any conversations within that remit. That is all, Sergeant Devreux. Dismiss!'

Florentine stiffened to attention, received her dismissal and smartly about-turned. Life was suddenly about to change dramatically. She was going home.

It was over two hours later when Angela Barclay joined Florentine. Like Florentine, she had a packed kit bag over her shoulder and a slightly shell-shocked look in her eyes.

'Wow! How was that for a surprise!' Angela greeted her. 'Don't let anyone ever say that service life is dull and monotonous!'

'Not in wartime, anyway!' Florentine amended, looking slightly anxiously at her friend. Angela's natural complexion was fairer that Florentine's but, like her friend, the hot summer had given her a golden tan. Her features were softly pretty and feminine; her short chestnut hair curling over the brim of her army cap. Her tawny eyes were filled with excitement, their tiny golden flecks giving the impression of the dancing flames of an open fire.

'Why is your island so important all of a sudden? I thought it was fairly small, only about twenty miles long, didn't you say?'

'Yes, but think of where it stands, partway between the fortresses of Royan and La Rochelle. It guards the entire coast along there, preventing the landing of Allied troops. If the Allied army could get control of the island, they could move much more quickly inland. We have to get it back.'

Their days of briefing were intense, exhausting their minds and bodies. Florentine was perturbed to hear that the Resistance movement on Île d'Oleron had been discontinued since early October of the previous year and was only just being reinstated, hence the need for some radio transmitters and receivers, and people able to use them. Many people she knew could have been drafted in to operate the radios but none, it seemed, with her knowledge of the island.

'We will take the transmitters with us?' she asked at one of the briefings.

'No. It would be too dangerous for you,' the officer replied. 'We'll get some over there as soon as we can by other couriers.'

'But, it will be just as dangerous for them, yes?'

'If they're caught, but they are more practised in guerrilla warfare than you are. If you're caught empty-handed, you may be able to bluff your way out of it but, if you were caught with radio transmitters and receivers, you would be shot immediately. We need you there to be ready to assist in using the transmitters when we get them out there.'

Their heads bursting with information, codes and plans, it was with some relief that, six days later, Florentine and Angela snuggled down in the shallow bottom of the small dark sailing boat that was to slip them ashore under the noses of the enemy.

Gone were all the signs of their military connection and modern living style. They were sombrely dressed in the hardwearing but simple skirts, blouses, jackets and shoes of the island's female population. To Florentine, it was a matter of stepping back three years. To Angela, now given the French form of her name, Angelique, it was more like forty or fifty years, to the days of her grandparents.

Florentine breathed in the fresh, salty air as deeply as she could without bursting her lungs. She peered through the darkness. Where were they? It was inky black. There was no moon, not even any stars. All were hidden by the thick cloud that had made this an ideal night for their silent journey.

The shallow-bottomed craft crept silently along the inland channel, its mariners carefully measuring the depth. It was a low tide, making their skills more needful as they moved into the shallow waters.

Florentine was breathless with anticipation. She knew where they were now. They had passed the mainland town of Marennes, and Bourcefranc, where the small ferry linked the mainland to the island, was slightly ahead. Any moment now they would swing westward towards the island into one of the main channels that led into the salines, the sea marshes of Le Petit Village and La Giraudiere where the oyster farmers made their living amongst the old rectangle, man-made salt lakes.

She glanced towards where she knew Angela's . . . Angelique's she corrected herself . . . blackened face would be as watchful as her own, though her friend was blissfully unaware of the danger from the sands and sea. Her attentive ears were listening only for sounds of man-made danger from any alert

German sentries.

There were none.

They were now in the shelter of the salines. The sails were silently lowered and the craft moved by poles driven down into the water, punting slowly forwards.

The low sound of the peewit cut through the air, answered in kind by the mariner in the bows. The boat shuddered to a stop as it grounded on the sandy bottom of the inlet and blackened hands reached out from the dry bank, holding fast the boat whilst Florentine, Angela and one of the mariners carefully stepped ashore.

With a low, 'Bon chance!' from both parties, the small craft immediately melted back into the blackness of the night.

Silently, half-crouched, they threaded their way through the maze of the salines, thankful for the ragged growth of vegetation that provided some sort of cover against an over-keen vigilance of enemy eyes.

Angela followed blindly, her mind now working on automatic pilot. She could feel her heart thumping painfully against her ribs, the sound as loud as the beat of horses' hooves in her inner ear. Was she really cut out for this? It was one thing crawling through rough terrain with a rifle slung over your shoulder on training exercises, and another thing altogether doing it for real.

The ground beneath their feet was firmer now. They were on a track of some kind. A hand reached backward pressing on to her shoulder and she instinctively crouched to the ground, her heart racing. The two behind her crouched also.

At first she couldn't hear anything then the steady hum of a motorised vehicle, its headlights slicing through the darkness, drifted through the night air. It had to be a German patrol vehicle. No friendly vehicles would advertise their presence like this.

The light seemed to hover above

them. They held their breath. Had they been seen?

It seemed not.

The vehicle and light passed.

They waited until the hum faded into silence once more and then continued their journey. Soon, they were amongst a number of small buildings. They flattened themselves into the wall, hands linked in a chain.

Angela bumped into the leader, hearing a quietly tapped tattoo. Her trained ears heard 'merle' and she smiled. 'Blackbird'. With their blackened faces, it was appropriate.

The door opened just wide enough for them to slip inside, once again into total darkness, and the door quietly snicked back into place. Only then did a dim light begin to glow, revealing half a dozen figures — five men of varying ages and a woman of middle years, her face and hands weather-beaten, her clothes rough spun.

The woman lifted her hands and cupped them about Angela's face, kissing her and then Florentine, saying over and over, 'Welcome, my little ones!' leaving the men to slap each other's backs as they shook hands.

'May I present my friend, Angelique, Madame Naud, messieurs?'

Florentine swung her glance over the men, vaguely recognising a couple.

'Bernard! Georges!'

Only then did she look closely at the blackened face of the man who had guided them through the salines. His eyes were full of merriment and she felt a surge of pleasure tingle through her.

'Pierre!'

2

The man stepped forward, his arms outstretched, a rueful smile now playing upon his lips.

'Sorry, Florentine. I'm afraid you must do with his younger brother. Hopefully, you will notice that I have grown up since you last saw me.'

He made an extravagant bow and took hold of her hand, bringing it to his lips, his dark eyes dancing.

'Charles St Clare, at your service, Mademoiselle Devreux. Your delightful face is truly enchanting, as usual!'

His eyes were fixed on her face. Even covered with smears of black oil, her striking beauty touched his heart and made it thud painfully inside his chest. No, she wasn't beautiful, he amended candidly . . . but she was striking. But then, he was biased. He had always been in love with her, even though he knew her heart and hopes lay with his brother.

Florentine laughed, now at ease. It was true . . . he had grown up! Get that black stuff off his face and he would be every bit as good-looking as his brother!

'I don't need a mirror to disprove your words!' she said lightly, as she stepped into the fond embrace the outstretched arms offered. They had roamed the local countryside together until teenage hormones had turned her heart to his handsome brother. But he was still her friend . . . a dear one, at that. She pulled free and reached out a hand to draw Angela forward.

'Angelique, come and meet Charles, a lifelong friend.'

Charles paid Angela a similar compliment and had the pleasure of seeing a pink blush creep into her cheeks under the black grease.

Florentine's heart leaped. Angela and Charles; herself and Pierre! Something good might yet come out of this ghastly war.

'Hey, daydreamer! Where are you?' Charles's teasing voice reached her.

Pulled back to the present, she smiled happily. Oh, it was good to see him again, and the others. She quickly asked about her parents and was thankful to be assured that they were well and still managing their family bakery in the small market town of Le Chateau. They had been told that she was coming to the island and she would see them tomorrow.

They spent some time passing on information from the mainland, poring over maps and being given a more detailed briefing of the work ahead. There would be dangers to face but the team was trained well and risks cut to a minimum.

There were so many questions Florentine wanted to ask, especially about Pierre. Where was he stationed? And why was Charles here? Surely he should be on the mainland with the Allied army. But she knew the questions would have to wait until another time. Their gathering was strictly illegal and, should they be detected, the rebirth of the Resistance would be delayed. One by one, the men slipped out into the night leaving Florentine and Angela to spend the night with Madame Naud.

The next morning, they awoke to the exultant cry of a cockerel and the more gentle sound of doves cooing, high up in the trees. Weak rays of early-morning sunshine streamed in through the curtains, even though it was not yet five o'clock . . . and the delicious smell of freshly-baked rolls of bread wafted into their bedroom.

'Heavenly bliss!' Angela decided. 'Let's get up.'

Madame Naud apologised for the lack of coffee and anything other than homemade butter to put on the rolls.

'It's better than what we're used to,' Florentine assured her, thinking of the dark rye bread and cheap margarine that had been their main breakfast fare for so long that they had forgotten what anything else tasted like.

As they spoke, a farm cart pulled by an ox lumbered to a stop outside the cottage. Its driver was Charles again. Whistling, he knocked on the door and entered smiling broadly.

As he saw the girls, he made a show of great surprise, accompanied by an elaborate bow.

'Mesdemoiselles! What beauties!' he said and began to look behind the chairs and into the corners. 'Where are those miserable-looking wenches I fetched here last night?'

'Miserable-looking wenches, indeed!' Florentine retorted. 'Who are you to talk? I can't think why I thought you were Pierre last night.'

Charles spread out his hands in mock defeat, directing his reply to Angela.

'Alas! She is correct! I live in the shadow of my handsome brother! All the girls swoon at his feet and they trample over me as they rush to his side, even my old playmate here!'

Angela laughed.

'I'm sure you are mistaken. You are very good-looking yourself.'

'Ah! An admirer at last! And one so beautiful.' Charles seized hold of her hand and raised it to his lips, his eyes dancing. 'I will love you for ever.'

Florentine grinned, agreeing secretly with Angela. The three years of absence had matured his looks and he was now the image of what Pierre had been. A few strands of his dark hair hung over his forehead and she had the strangest urge to reach out her hand to tidy them away.

An unexpected twinge to her heart confused her. She suddenly wasn't sure that she wanted her friend to attract Charles's affections after all. He had always shown a fondness for her, even though she had never encouraged him beyond friendship.

'How is Pierre, by the way?' she asked casually. 'Is he still around?'

'You see, Angelique, she has me in the flesh yet she asks after Pierre! The sooner I get the guy married the better it will be for me.'

Florence's heart skipped a beat. Pierre was still unmarried then.

She shrugged carelessly.

'I just wondered. You can bring me up to date on all our friends. I haven't heard from many since the war started.'

'Later,' Charles promised. 'We must be on our way. It's getting late.'

He held open the door to allow Florentine and Angela to step outside.

'Wear your shawl and don't make yourselves look attractive,' he told them as they approached the cart, laden with farm produce ready for market. 'You must never draw attention to yourselves. It could mean danger.'

He handed them up on to the front driving seat, Angela first, to sit in the middle, Florentine next to her.

'The aim is to blend into the background as much as possible,' he continued as he went round to the driver's side. 'If we meet with any patrols pretend to be half-asleep and if we are stopped leave the talking to me.

They know me well.'

He dropped his jaw and made his eyes cross over slightly.

'The Germans think me an imbecile, of no use to the French army.'

'At least you don't need to act,' Florentine said tartly, but her grin softened her words.

They travelled in silence for a few minutes and Florentine temporarily forgot about the war . . . the fighting . . . the killing. She was back on her beloved island. She breathed in deeply, filling her lungs with the scent of the mimosa blossom that continually drifted over the island. The rapidly-warming sun seemed to heat the small yellow buds, causing them to explode their fragrance into the air.

The rays of the sun felt deliciously warm upon her skin, reminding her of her carefree days as a child, running barelegged along the shore and through the cornfields.

The larks were singing high in the sky, unmindful of the human misery that held the islanders in bondage upon their own soil.

The thought brought Florentine back to the present and she bobbed her head around Angela, longing to learn more about Pierre.

'Go on, then! Tell me about our friends. Who's doing what?'

Charles met her eyes briefly but turned back to concentrate on the road before answering.

'It is not good. Most of the lads are in the army. Guillaume was killed in action, also Thierry and Vincent. Many of the girls, like you, were drafted into the army, though some remained behind. A number of us guys were drafted back to the island soon after the occupation, supposedly medically unfit for service. Do you remember Alexie and Denis, a couple of years older than us? And Robert and Marcel? And many others. Pierre soon joined us.'

Florentine caught her breath. So, he was here!

A faint flicker of Charles's eyes

showed he had noted her reaction, but he continued without a break.

'We were smuggled in, as you have been, and gradually integrated back into the island society. In reality, we were an underground unit, divided amongst a dozen or so groups of older patriots.'

His attention sharpened and he hissed a swift command.

'Put your shawl back on, Florentine!'

Florentine bristled. He really was the bossiest man she had ever met! No wonder she had always favoured Pierre!

Within seconds they heard a vehicle approaching and, as Florentine hastily pulled her shawl over her head, a German army vehicle swung round the corner a hundred yards or so ahead of them.

'Ignore them!' Charles muttered sharply. 'If they want to investigate, they must find somewhere to turn their vehicle around.'

He allowed the beast to solidly plod on its way, hunching his shoulders in indolent fashion. The girls were slouched against each other as though half asleep. As they drew level, a sudden movement from Charles caused Florentine to glance sideways past Angela to him. He was grinning idiotically at the soldiers as their vehicle passed by and she marvelled at his audacity.

They could tell that the vehicle had halted a few yards behind them and held their breath, expecting a command to halt, but it didn't come.

'They see me every day,' Charles reminded them in undertones. 'They call me Stupid Oaf! At least, that's what I think it means!'

A fleeting grin gave way to a more serious expression.

'There will be more soldiers about,' he warned. 'They come to the market and make their presence felt. Don't do anything to encourage them to challenge you. You must always look defeated, dejected.'

The track was narrow and meandering, wending its way past the beds of the old salt marshes where the salt farmers used to allow the sea to flood the dug-out rectangular plots and then block the exit. The hot sun would then evaporate the water, leaving behind the salt deposits, ready to be collected.

'The trade has revived,' Charles commented, noticing her glance. 'It's one less thing to import or smuggle over, and it gives us ready access to the marshes. The more we have reason to move about the island, the easier it is for us to keep track of all they are doing. There isn't much going on that we don't know about.'

'What has been happening here?' Florentine asked. 'Has there been much fighting? I haven't heard any details.'

'Not much. The Germans swiftly swarmed over the island, taking each town in turn and leaving a group of soldiers in charge. They put batteries all around the Atlantic coast, at Le Grand Village, Vert-bois, Domino, Boyardville, everywhere.' His voice was bitter, as he rhymed off the familiar place-names.

'That's why we brought you in from the mainland. So far, they seem to think they are safe from there.'

Florentine pondered what he had said, trying to imagine the beaches she had loved now decorated with concrete bunkers and barbed-wire.

'Did people not resist?'

'They didn't have much chance. They were mainly too old or too young. It was different, of course, after we had been smuggled back in. Once we had got organised, we aimed to cause as much inconveniences and delays as we could. We succeeded, until the eleventh of October last year, when the Gestapo arrived. Being under an occupation army was bad enough, but things became decidedly worse after the Gestapo came. Then . . . '

His face changed. His lips tightened and his eyes lost their sparkle.

Florentine thought he wasn't going to continue, but after a deep sigh, he did.

'An operation went wrong. The

Gestapo were waiting for us. There was a battle. Alexie, Thomas and Claude were killed, Denis was wounded. The rest of us fled, but they knew where to find our leaders. Robert Etchebarne, Pierre Weihn, Pierre Balluret and Clotaire Perdriaux were arrested, others, later. The first two leaders were shot at Bordeaux. The other two died in transit.'

Florentine had known most of the people Charles had mentioned. It was hard to think that some were now dead. But, wasn't that the same all over France, and other European countries, wherever the war had touched?

'We were betrayed,' Charles said at length. 'That was the hardest thing to bear. Betrayed by one of our own people.'

Florentine could understand his bitterness.

'Yes, they said so at our briefing, but who would do that? What reason would they have?'

Charles laughed bitterly.

'Money! Protection! Immunity! Fear! Who knows?'

'Someone must know! Has no-one tried to find out?' Florentine leaned forward, looking around Angela, who had listened to all this in silence.

Charles's eyes were bleak as he returned her gaze, but he did not speak. Somehow, Florentine knew there was more to come, but not yet.

They were on the outskirts of Le Chateau now, passing through one of the former gateways of the historic town walls that had been breached in battles of long ago, heading for the daily market where they were taking the farm produce.

'Do not mention what we have been talking about in the market,' Charles warned quietly. 'It is a very sore subject and has caused much division amongst us.'

They had turned into the town square, merging with other carts and people on foot, exchanging greetings. Florentine recognised some, but they

32

had been tutored well and none showed any surprise at her presence. It was as if she had never been away.

The main market hall was a square building made of stone. It had a wide entrance on all of the four sides, with market stalls set around the edges and in the centre. It was to one of the centre stalls that Charles directed Florentine and Angelique to carry the heavy woven baskets filled with fruit and vegetables.

Stalls vending oysters, mussels and a variety of fish were being filled by some of the local fishermen. Florentine looked around, noticing many empty stalls — the butcher's stall, the cheeses, the wines and . . .

'Papa!'

There he was, watching her with a bemused smile on his face, waiting for her to notice him. With a swift glance around to make sure no soldiers were about, he held wide his arms and she flew into them. He crushed her to him.

It was a brief reunion. A nudge from a passing shopper reminded them to curb their greetings and they parted reluctantly.

Oh, it was good to see him! She would see Maman later and would sleep in her own bed tonight. Bliss!

Just as she was thinking that it was just like the old days, a heavy tramping of boots and a change in people's demeanour warned of enemy presence. Grey uniformed soldiers entered the market with a swagger and arrogantly shouldered people out of their way. They picked up items of vegetables and tossed them down in disdain, picking up others and eventually choosing what they wanted. Florentine saw no money change hands but none of the stallholders objected.

She was still standing by her father's bread stall and was startled to realise that a fresh-faced soldier was addressing her. She didn't understand the words but his meaning was clear. He was asking for the loaf he held in his hands. Her heart thumped as she surreptitiously glanced at her father. A slight movement of his eyes indicated that she give assent, so she shrugged her shoulders and tried to look unconcerned as she made no move to refuse him.

A second soldier, standing a pace behind him, said something and laughed crudely and the first soldier seemed embarrassed. He clicked his heels together and bowed stiffly before executing a smart about-turn and strode away.

'Come behind the stall, Florentine!' her father commanded.

Florentine was happy to obey, noticing that Angela was already within one of the centre stalls efficiently arranging the farm produce for sale. She could sense that Charles was watching her severely. Well, it hadn't been her fault the soldier had addressed her!

Trading soon became brisk as local people came to buy their daily provisions and it was mid-morning before a slight lull gave Florentine the opportunity to glance over to the vegetable stall. She was just in time to see Angela's eyes widen slightly and a blush decorate her cheeks. Florentine had never seen her look so beautiful as she did at that moment.

But it was the rapt expression in her eyes that caused her to wonder who had caused the facial transformation. She swung her head to follow the direction of Angela's captivated glance, totally unprepared for the shock to come.

Angela was looking at a tall, dark-haired young man, who had a similar enraptured expression on his face.

Florentine's heart flared into life . . . and just as quickly sank again as her mind made sense of what she was witnessing.

It was Pierre St Clare!

Florentine had known of people who said that they had fallen in love at first sight, but she had never given it much credence. How could it be? Love was more than physical attraction. But, from the way that Angela and Pierre were looking at each other, Florentine knew they had instantaneously and irrevocably fallen in love.

3

Florentine felt desolate. Yet she bore no antipathy towards her friend. How could she when she had witnessed that incredulous surge of joy that passed between Pierre and Angela? Pierre had never looked at her like that! Nor at anyone else, as far as she knew. For all she had idolised him, she hadn't been blind to his arrogance towards the girls who fell at his feet. He took their adulation as his right.

Florentine watched as he moved forward, his eyes never wavering from Angela's face. She saw him stop in front of her and then glance towards Charles to be introduced. She watched as Pierre's lips moved to say how enchanted he was to make her acquaintance, adding, 'You will always be my special angel,' as his left hand picked up Angela's hand and drew it to his lips.

How often she had dreamed of him saying similar words to her!

She saw Charles look across in her direction and she forced a smile on to her face, hoping it didn't look as brittle as it felt. She turned to her father.

'There is Pierre, Papa. I must go and say hello to him.'

Jacques Devreux frowned. His eyes flickered anxiously around the market but could see no soldiers. He relaxed slightly but, even so, looked none too pleased.

'This isn't the time or place, Florentine,' he warned quietly.

'I'm only going to say hello, for heaven's sake!' she protested.

Really, did her father think he had to protect her from Pierre's womanising ways? She could deal with this herself, and she wanted to get it over and done with. And it would be best to do it here where she could make an early excuse to move away.

'I said, not now! You are supposed to be quietly reintegrating yourself back into the community, not throwing yourself at the first young man you see!'

'I'm not! Besides, there are no soldiers here at the moment.'

Without giving her father the chance to say more, she slipped out from behind the bakery stall and made straight for Pierre and Angela. Her heart was beating fast, a smile fixed on her face.

'Hello, Pierre. It's good to see you. You've met Angelique, I see.'

She smiled brightly at Angela.

'I told you he has an eye for a pretty girl. He's a rogue! Don't believe a word he says!'

She said it teasingly and was relieved to see Angela smile happily.

All Florentine wanted was to get the next few minutes over and done with. She made herself meet Charles's eyes, determined to convince him of her indifference to Pierre's preference of her friend.

'Will I be seeing you later, Charles? You didn't quite finish bringing me up to date with everything.'

Charles looked distinctly annoyed.

'I will see you later, but get back to your father. I told you not to draw attention to yourself.' His voice was cold and quiet; his eyes full of derision.

'I'll return when I'm ready!' she hissed back. 'You're not my keeper!'

'That's where you are mistaken,' Charles said quietly, his lips hardly moving so that no-one could lip-read his words. 'Get back immediately or else I will have you removed from the island before you have time to turn round. Your behaviour is a danger to us all.'

With a sinking heart, Florentine realised she had reacted foolishly. She had gone against the briefing they had been given. She looked around. The townsfolk portrayed a studious lack of interest in their conversation but she sensed that it was a sham. They were all aware that she was betraying her recent arrival on the island. Her flare of rebellion was replaced by a feeling of shame. Her cheeks flushed red.

'I'm sorry!' she muttered and fled back to the bread stall, wanting the ground to swallow her up from their sight.

Her father said nothing. He was serving a customer and, when the transaction was made he handed her some francs and an empty basket.

'Go and buy some vegetables and take them home to your mother. She will be pleased to see you,' he added, implying that no-one else was!

Thoroughly ashamed with herself and blinking back tears of contrition, Florentine did as she was bidden. There was no sign of Angela and Pierre. They had quietly left the scene. She avoided Charles by going to the other end of his vegetable stall and making her purchases from Madame Aubry, who had worked for the St Clare family for years.

Head down, she swiftly made her way through the network of narrow streets, neatly set out centuries ago within the town walls. Suddenly, she regretted having accepted the mission and her return to the island. She was obviously totally unsuited to the underground mission and the sooner she was able to leave, the better. She would request a transfer as soon as she was able. Everyone concerned would be better off without her, anyway.

A pang of distress hit her. How ashamed her parents would be.

She hardly noticed where she was going. It was a journey she had made many times every day until she had left the island. Her parents lived on the outer perimeter of the town near the site of the former port of earlier centuries, long laid idle by the present-day port. More hollyhocks bordered the doorway of their home, softening the glare of the noonday sun as it bounced back off the walls into her eyes.

The inside of the house seemed dark and gloomy after the brightness outside, though she knew it wasn't really so. It wasn't a large house and most of the ground floor was taken up by the bake-house. The smell of freshly-baked bread from the hot ovens broke through her self-imposed barrier of a mixture of resentment and shame and, as her mother lifted her head from where she was rolling out a large rectangle of pastry, she burst into tears.

Beatrice Devreux let out a cry of pleasure and concern and enveloped Florentine in her welcoming arms.

'Oh, ma petite! Ma petite!' she cried out, her own tears running into her daughter's abundant hair.

Taking Florentine's tears to be tears of joy at being home, no awkward questions were asked, other than about her journey and arrival on the island and, after some fresh bread and a drink of weak coffee, Florentine went up the stairs to her bedroom. It seemed just as she had left it.

Its walls were painted cream and it had a well-worn square of red carpet on the floor. The yellow checked gingham curtains were the same ones she had left there and a few ornaments from her teenage years adorned the small bedside cupboard.

From the small multi-paned window, Florentine could see the sea and out across towards the mainland as far as Rochefort. The sea was bright blue, reflecting the summer sky. All reminders of war seemed far removed and Florentine wished she were able to return to the carefree days of her childhood. She rested her folded arms upon the sill and gazed out. The tranquil familiarity of the scene brought a sense of peace to her heart and a sense of proportion to her mind.

She heard sounds indicating that her father had arrived home and, deciding to face his wrath sooner rather than later, she splashed some water on to her face and rubbed it dry with her towel. She picked up her brush and ran it through her hair and then fastened it back off her face with a piece of ribbon that lay in her drawer.

Satisfied with her reflection, she ran

lightly down the stairs. To her relief and surprise, her father made no mention of her behaviour in the market. As they ate their simple mid-day meal of baked mussels and fresh bread, she told them as much as she felt was common knowledge about her life in the Allied forces and a brief résumé of her journey to the island, describing Angela, to be called Angelique, she reminded them, to her mother, adding lightly, with a sidelong, apprehensive glance at her father, 'And she seems to have caught the eye of Pierre St Clare already! He's a fast worker, I'll give him that!'

'Well, I hope you're over your crush on him! His brother, Charles, is a much more suitable boy!' her mother asserted forcefully.

'Maman! We are no longer boys and girls! We have grown up!'

Beatrice sighed. 'Ah, too quickly forced to! And many youngsters have not been given the chance to grow up, just as in the previous generation.' She shook her head sadly, remembering the losses of the First World War. 'I pray it will soon be over.'

Finding it hard to remain inactive inside the house, Florentine asked if it were safe to go and sit on one of the beaches.

'Nowhere is completely safe,' Jacques commented, 'but the Germans are not in heavy numbers here. They are mainly farther up the island. We try to carry on much of our life as normal. Just don't make yourself conspicuous. Do you understand the German language?'

'A little, but nowhere near fluent.'

'Keep your papers on you and show them when asked.'

★   ★   ★

It was the hour of the afternoon siesta and the streets were almost deserted. Florentine went down to the sea, to a quiet spot she knew in the shelter of the citadel wall and the natural rock formation at the northern end of the town.

It was there that Charles eventually found her. He clambered over the rocks and stood over her where she sat with her back against the sea wall, staring ahead of her towards the quietly lapping sea. He knew she hadn't heard him approach and he delayed speaking to her, letting the picture of her quiet musings imprint itself upon his mind, wondering if he would ever be able to tell her how much he loved her and longed for her love in return.

He had left the market with a heavy heart, not wanting to face the fact that his hopes that after three years of absence, things would be different between him and Florentine, that she would at last see him with open eyes, had proved to be false. Her eyes were still blinded by her one-sided, teenage love for Pierre.

He understood how she felt, because didn't he feel the same way about her? He didn't blame Pierre for her blind attachment. Pierre had never encouraged her. He had had too many available local beauties to choose from, to even consider saving himself for a long-absent young admirer.

Charles had often wondered if Pierre would ever settle down and marry. He wondered what it had been that had sparked so vibrantly between Pierre and Angelique. Whatever it was, he wished it would spark between himself and Florentine, but he was beginning to think that it never would. He had lived for too long in his elder brother's shadow.

Even so, he didn't want her to get hurt, and he knew that she would if she persisted in throwing herself at Pierre's feet. If that look of utter belonging that had passed between Pierre and Angelique burned deeply, Pierre wouldn't even notice Florentine.

He would trample her underfoot and be totally unaware that he had done so.

Others would notice though — and that hurt him. Others had seen her jealousy and her attempt to warn off her friend — and neither action was worthy of her.

How he wished he could loosen the piece of ribbon that held her hair off her face and run his fingers through its luxurious tresses. He could almost feel its silky smoothness on his fingers and they tingled in anticipation.

'I knew I would find you here.'

His voice, when he finally spoke, was flat and had a cold edge to it. He refused her invitation to sit beside her and remained standing over her. It was the only way he could deal with the situation.

Florentine didn't look up at him. She hugged her knees and continued to look out to sea. Having had time to think over the events of the morning, she decided that it was up to her to clear the air between them.

'I'm sorry about this morning,' she apologised contritely. 'I can see now that I was out of order and could have landed myself in trouble.'

Charles felt incensed by her words.

He knew he was over-reacting but a white-hot fire seemed to rage within him.

'Landed yourself in trouble! Is that all you care about? You could have landed every one of us in trouble, all because you couldn't bear to see your friend get attention from Pierre! How selfish can you be?'

'I'm sorry?'

It was a question, not a repeat apology, though Charles seemed to think it was.

'And so you should be! I would never have believed it if I hadn't witnessed it for myself. Rushing over like that the minute Pierre looks at another girl, one far prettier than yourself, if you are in any doubt, and trying to put her off him! 'Always has an eye for a pretty girl, and don't believe a word he says'!' his voice mimicked.

Florentine flushed at his accurate mimicry of her words, but was horrified at his misinterpretation of them. 'But, I didn't . . . '

'Don't try to deny it! I was there, remember!'

'No! She's my friend!'

'Was!' he corrected. 'I doubt if she'll want to know you after that little demonstration of jealousy!'

'I'm not jealous!' She leaped to her feet and faced him angrily.

'Yes, you are! You've always carried a torch for him. Your whole school knew it, and half of the ones left around have already made a point of telling Angel so.'

'Oh! 'Angel', is it? Are you smitten, too?'

She couldn't help it. His words had hurt and she wanted him to hurt, too.

'Did your better-looking brother move in too fast for you? I remember what you said last night. 'I'll love you for ever.' You were all over her. I'm surprised you didn't snatch her up and kiss her properly. Or, don't you know how?'

Charles's face flushed angrily.

'Like this, do you mean?'

Before Florentine had time to register what he had said, Charles had cupped her face with his hands and pulled her towards him, roughly covering her lips with his own.

Initially, Florentine struggled to free herself but, as the kiss deepened, a change came over her so suddenly that she was powerless to resist. Her lips tingled with an intensity she had never experienced and she wanted more of him.

A spiralling sensation of melting heat seemed to flow through her body and she found herself moulding her body to his, her hands reaching up to entwine her fingers in his hair, holding his head close to her in case he should think of ending the kiss.

It was only when they both made a small moan of desire that they sprang apart, shaken by the intensity of their need. Florentine found herself breathless, her heart pounding.

'Was that me you were kissing, or Pierre?' Charles asked unwisely, knocked for six by their kiss and hardly able to believe it had been as it was.

Florentine felt shattered by the remark. It had been like the awakening of her soul, relegating all other dalliances to the obscurity of ordinariness.

Pierre had never kissed her, but Charles didn't know that.

'There was no comparison,' she now said coldly. 'Pierre knows how to kiss a girl properly. He's not a novice like that. And he treats his girls more honourably.'

'Huh! More honourable, is he? I doubt if the Resistance would agree with you.'

As soon as he had said the words, Florentine could tell that he wished he hadn't . . . and the words pulled her up sharply.

'What has the Resistance got to do with it? There is no question about Pierre's honour, is there?'

Charles turned away, preparing to leap up on to the sea wall, intending to bring the conversation to a close.

'This has gone far enough. I only came to tell you that if you want to stay on the island, you had better get it into your head that our oath of allegiance is as binding as that of the Allies, and our leaders will not tolerate disobedience in any form. You are to attend a meeting tonight, so make sure you get some sleep this afternoon. I will come for you at eleven o'clock.'

But Florentine wasn't to be side-tracked so easily. She grabbed hold of his arm and swung him back to face her.

'What did you mean about Pierre?'

At his refusal to answer, her eyes narrowed slightly.

'I'll only ask someone else if you won't say.'

Charles felt a chill run through him. He hadn't meant this to happen. He considered her threat and knew that she meant it.

Somehow, she knew what he was going to say — and her heart screamed against it. When he spoke, his voice betrayed his emotion.

'With regard to the betrayal last October, there are four main suspects,' he admitted quietly. 'Paul, Hubert, André . . . and Pierre.'

4

Florentine stared at him angrily. Even though she had known what he was about to say, she couldn't accept it. It wasn't true! It couldn't be!

'You are despicable!' she accused him harshly. 'And you talk of me being jealous! No-one in their right mind would believe that about Pierre.'

She began to clamber back over the sea-wall.

Charles leaped after her. He caught hold of her arm and pulled her back on to the beach.

'Will you stand still and listen to the whole story?' he shouted at her. 'I don't believe it either! No-one does, really, but the situation is there. Someone betrayed us. He was the one who had the better opportunity.'

'Then concentrate on the others.'

'War does things to people, Florentine. It changes them.'

'Not Pierre.'

'He has changed, though, since he was discharged from the Allied Forces. He saw some dreadful sights. We all did.'

Florentine considered his words.

'What do you mean, discharged from the Forces? Why was he discharged? Wasn't it to come back here, like you?'

'Not really. He was discharged before that, after his injury.'

'What sort of injury?'

'Didn't you notice? I thought you had eyes for no-one else. His right arm is useless. It just hangs at his side. He can't fire a rifle or fight one hundred per cent. So, he was discharged.'

Florentine felt a searing shock slice through her. She had been so caught up with her own reaction to Pierre's presence in the market that she hadn't even noticed his disability.

'Poor Pierre. Being best at everything was all he was interested in.'

They parted, still on bitter terms. Florentine felt furious about what Charles had said about Pierre. How dare he accuse her of jealousy and then act like that towards his brother? How two-faced could he get?

Her parents were having their mid-day siesta when she returned to her home but, as soon as they were awake, she asked about Pierre. Her father looked uncomfortable.

'We do not talk of it,' he reproved her.

'If I am to be working with him, I need to know.'

Beatrice agreed.

'You must tell her, Jacques.'

'You don't need to know all the details, just that only the team who were to go out that night knew where they were going. André, Hubert, Paul and Pierre had all been stopped for questioning earlier in the day and Pierre was seen returning later, after some details had been changed.'

'That proves nothing!'

'Maybe not, but information was given and lives were lost. Is it any easier to believe it was André or Paul or Hubert?'

'No, but I feel like a traitor just talking about it.'

'That is what war does to people, Florentine. It makes us all suspicious of our neighbours. So, take care whom you speak to and what you say.'

'And who might be listening,' Beatrice added, touching the tip of her tongue. 'We learn to watch it.'

Florentine had the grace to blush. She had her lapse of carelessness still to answer for at the meeting with some of the island's appointed leaders. She wasn't looking forward to it.

The meeting, later that night, wasn't as bad as she feared. Charles came as promised and, dressed in her darkest clothes, she followed him in silence through the dark streets and down a narrow alleyway. They met no enemy soldiers but her heart was pounding as they slipped from shadow to shadow.

Charles scratched quietly on the wooden door and it opened silently to admit them inside. Only three men were present besides Charles. Florentine had known them all her life.

One of them, Clément Videau, the leader of the group at Le Chateau, spoke gravely to her about the dangers of careless talk and then, amidst nods of agreement from the others, agreed to overlook her lapse with a cautionary warning.

'Charles, we want you to take Mademoiselle Devreux on some night-time exercises to initiate her into the work of our unit.'

Videau turned back to Florentine.

'You must take heed of what he tells you, mademoiselle. The most dangerous time for you will be these next few weeks. If you get through these, you will stand a good chance of getting through the rest of the war. Charles is one of our most experienced men.'

Florentine refused to meet Charles's eyes. She was sure he would be smirking triumphantly. This was no time to announce petty grievances about him and his mistreatment of her. Unbidden, the memory of their kiss on the seashore leaped into her mind. Her lips tingled at the remembrance and the fingers of her right hand involuntarily touched them.

She was startled when Charles touched her arm, wondering if he had been aware of her thoughts.

He hadn't, but his thoughts weren't too dissimilar. From where he stood, slightly behind her, he could see the elegant line of her neck and the upward tilt of her chin. He could imagine the velvet smoothness of her lips, their softness still imprinted in his mind. Feeling shaken by his thoughts, he tore his glance away and took strict control of himself. His voice was quite brusque when he spoke.

'Come on, then. You may as well start at once. We have some reconnoitring to do.'

Florentine pulled herself together.

'Where are we going?'

'For tonight we'll work around the citadel. There's something going on there and we need to know what it is.'

One of the men handed her a pair of black trousers and a balaclava for her to put on.

'These will be better for you to wear, Mademoiselle Florentine. Go behind the screen to change.'

She did as she was bidden and, when she re-emerged, Charles had already pulled another balaclava over his own head.

Once outside again, Florentine could hardly see Charles in order to follow him. She hesitated, unsure of her bearings. Charles realised this and reached backwards to take hold of her hand.

His touch seemed to send an electric current through her arm and she instinctively jerked her hand away from him. Just what did he think he was up to?

'Get hold of me!' he hissed in her ear.

'How else can you follow me? We can't hang around until your eyes are accustomed to the dark! Oh, hang on to my jacket then!'

Finding that more acceptable, she did so and they silently slipped through the streets of the town heading towards the walled area of the citadel, a fortified bastion dating from the seventeenth century that had given the town its name. It had fallen into a state of semi-disrepair long since but was still a usable building.

By the time they reached its outer walls, Florentine could vaguely see their shape looming high above them. She tried to remember the lay-out from her childhood days of playing in the area, knowing that the moat was still filled with water in some places.

They crept up to the wall and flattened themselves against it. She had long since let go of Charles's jacket and now both her black-gloved hands were spread behind her on the rough stonework. After glancing quickly to both sides, they swiftly moved to the right. Florentine could remember that, through an archway along there, some stone steps led down to a lower level that they had pretended was a dungeon in their childhood games.

Some stones rattled above them. Had a night bird landed on the wall or was there someone on the higher level? Were the Germans also reconnoitring it? They waited to see if the sound was repeated, but all was now silent. Florentine felt herself relax. It was most likely some night-time creature out hunting, but they couldn't be sure.

If there were any German soldiers present, they were neither there in force nor in a settled capacity. They were doing the same as her and Charles, playing a game of cat and mouse, but why didn't they challenge them? It must be that they weren't sure who they were, or that they were out on exercise, with more than one group. Were they going to get caught in the middle?

They had investigated the stairways to some underground cells overlooking the moat and some other passages that led up to the outer walls on the inland side of the citadel. Charles signalled Florentine to stay where she was whilst he slipped up the stairway to check it out. It was eerie left alone in the darkness.

She was thankful when Charles rejoined her. The touch of his hand sent a tremor of relief coursing through her, but the depth of her reaction startled her, intensified when the warmth of his breath fanned across her cheek as he breathed, 'OK,' in her ear, signalling that they moved on.

She was no longer sure whether her heart was pounding with pent-up tension or her reaction to Charles's close presence and it took all of her concentration to push the troublesome thoughts away and concentrate on the task in hand. They swiftly crossed the southern entrance and flattened themselves against the wall again, anticipating a challenge that never came.

Next was a strongly-fortified underground cell that she remembered as having only two narrow slits in its outer wall. Charles indicated that they exchanged rôles and, holding her breath, she slipped into the total darkness. Freezing her body, she flattened herself against the wall and listened intently for the sound of breathing, aware that, if anyone else were present, he or she would know that she had entered the small space.

Detecting nothing, she relaxed slightly and slowly crept around the perimeter of the cell. It was empty. She reached the doorway and slipped into the passageway.

Charles was not there!

Where had he gone? Her brain slipped into active alert mode. He had either moved on to investigate farther or had been totally overpowered by persons unknown and taken away. Her commonsense told her that the latter was unlikely. She would have heard something. No-one could have over-powered him in total silence. He must have moved on to investigate something.

Carefully controlling her breathing, she silently moved forward. Keeping close to the wall, she silently mounted the external stone steps, neither seeing anyone nor hearing anything. Her mind continually envisaged the layout of the citadel as she ran in a stooped position to the far side of the building. There she paused again, listening intently. It served no purpose to stay up on the wall. Dark though it was, there was a slight lightening of the sky and a person would be faintly silhouetted against it. She silently descended a staircase to ground level and paused again.

There was still neither sight nor sound of Charles. Where had he got to? Was he deliberately testing her? But, what if it weren't so simple? What if he really had been apprehended by enemy hands? She couldn't risk it.

There were more cells to her right. They needed to be investigated before she could double back to check on those already done. She moved silently and systematically around that section of the citadel, carefully checking each aperture and cell, detecting nothing.

She had almost circumnavigated the whole inner structure. There was just another internal staircase that led down to a lower level under the gatehouse. There was an inner cell off the main one, but there was no way out. Once inside, she could be trapped. Would it be better to get out in safety herself or to continue in the hope of finding out what had happened to Charles?

All she knew was that she couldn't simply abandon him. She slipped inside the first narrow stone archway and listened. Was that a sound? She listened again. A stone rattled softly behind her. She half-turned, the hairs on her neck standing out. She knew that there was an alcove a few steps ahead and slid into it silently. Only someone who knew the citadel well would know it was there. She held her breath, sensing rather than hearing that someone was approaching. Not daring to breathe, she froze completely, aware of someone silently passing by. Then, silence, nothing but inky blackness. She let out her breath slowly and breathed in some more. If she waited until whoever it was had gone down the steps to the inner cell, she would be able to slip back outside and decide what to do next, unless there were more outside.

She eased herself out of the aperture and glided the few steps to the outer archway, keeping her back against the wall, listening intently before easing her body around the right-hand edge of the wall.

A faint scratching sound to her right sent her body into reverse but, instead of slipping back into the archway swiftly, she stepped back into the softness of an upright body. As her arms were pinioned to her sides from behind her, a bright beam shone into her eyes blinding her to everything else and a German voice snapped some sort of question.

Florentine's heart felt as if it had stopped beating.

She was caught!

5

More low-toned German voices seemed to surround her suddenly. An unseen hand ripped off her balaclava and a number of guttural voices made raucous comment. A hand stroked her cheek and Florentine did the only thing at her disposal. She hit out in the general direction of where she presumed the hand to have come from.

A harsh exclamation showed her sense of direction to have been near enough to cause offence, followed by a slap across her face. It was all the more a shock because she had been unable to anticipate it, her eyes still blinded by the strong beam of light.

Another sharp command made her captor tighten the grip on her arms, pulling them farther behind her. A tight band was fastened around her eyes and she felt herself being propelled forward.

Unable to resist, she stumbled along, losing track of how far she was taken, though she knew they were still within the walls of the citadel.

She heard a door being opened and was thrust inside, her arms still held tightly. More German words were spoken but she didn't recognise any of them. As a voice commanded her to sit, she was pushed on to a hard chair and her arms now bound around the back of it.

There followed a long period of rapid-fire questions, some in German, some translated into broken French, all demanding information — her name, her reason for being there, her accomplices, where she lived, how long she had been on the island, what she knew about the current activities of all the armed forces.

'I know nothing!'

Another voice took over, this time a French voice, speaking more kindly, coaxing her with promises of leniency if she co-operated with their questioning, offering a drink of water and a rest if she wished. The offer was tempting, but, at what cost. She shook her head and repeated the same sentence.

'I know nothing!'

The same voice praised her beauty, suggesting ways in which it might be marred. A cut here, a slash there . . . such a pity to disfigure her so, the voice said in silky tones as if he were offering her beauty treatment.

Florentine refused to answer.

Suddenly, the questioning stopped. Bewildered by the constant darkness and the sudden silence, she listened intently, coming to the conclusion that she was now alone. Her questioners had melted away silently into the darkness. She pulled at her bonds but they held fast. What now?

She tried to keep track of time but lost count. She reckoned it must have been about ten minutes later when the door opened.

'Florentine! You poor dear!'

She felt hands tugging at the knots

that held her to the chair, trying to loosen them, but failing.

'I cannot undo the knots. I need something sharp.'

'Angel . . . ique?' Florentine remembered to use the French name just in time. 'Is that you? Take off my blindfold.'

Florentine blinked in the dim light as it fell away. They were in what seemed like a store-room with bare stone walls and a stone floor. Apart from the chair she was seated upon, there was no other furniture in the room.

'It was terrible!' Angela exclaimed, crouching down in front of her, so that Florentine could see her properly.

'All those questions! But they said we can go soon.'

'You didn't tell them anything, did you?' Florentine asked sharply.

Angela laughed shakily.

'No, of course not, but it was hard not to. Who were you with?'

Tired though Florentine was, she frowned at Angela's questions and shook her head warningly at her.

'You know I can't tell you that. We're not free yet, you know!'

She glanced around and shivered. The room was empty apart from the two of them but others could be listening. She saw a gleam of something in Angela's eyes but before she could determine what it was, Angela was backing away.

'I've got to go,' she said. 'I'll try to get something to cut the rope.'

Angela disappeared through the doorway leaving Florentine on her own again. Feeling perturbed by Angela's actions, she tried to figure out what had happened.

The door opened again. This time it was Charles, smiling rather ruefully.

'That'll do for the present,' he said, flicking open a small pocket-knife and stepping behind her to saw at her bonds. 'You did pretty well, for a beginner!'

'Pardon?'

Florentine's relief that he was safe,

mixed with annoyance that it had all been a set-up, faded when it occurred to her that she still didn't really know if it were safe for her to speak. What if Charles were under duress to get her to talk, as it had seemed Angela was?

'Who are you?' she asked, her eyes narrowing slightly, sending him the unspoken message that he had better watch out if this were his idea of some sort of joke!

He laughed

'It's all right! You really can speak now. Come in, you guys. Convince her that it was a training exercise.'

Five or six young men stepped into the room, grinning sheepishly, aware of her anger, having gone through it all themselves on previous occasions.

'Thanks a lot!' Florentine said sarcastically. 'You frightened me out of my wits!'

'It was necessary!' one defended their actions. 'It is better to learn amongst friends, when you can be corrected. If it had been for real, you would be dead, or wishing you were, by now.'

'Hmm!' She conceded the point. 'And which one of you slapped me?'

'The one you hit!' Charles informed her. 'We had to make it real, otherwise it would have been a waste of time. One thing you failed on. You shouldn't have tried to find me. It would have been better to lose one agent than possibly two. The mission must take precedence.'

Florentine caught her breath. Could she have abandoned him? She doubted it, unless she knew without doubt that he was dead!

Would he have abandoned her? She had to accept that he would.

While that fact was slipping into her mind, she noticed Angela was joining them, now grinning broadly.

'You tried to get me to speak!' Florentine accused her, her sense of humour coming to the fore and accepting the night's events in their true light.

'You didn't, though!'

'No.'

'And you did better than me.'

'How did you do on the grilling?'

'About the same as you! No hard feelings?'

'No.' She was rubbing her wrists and flexing her arms, trying to get some use back into them. The men had gathered together and were discussing some further plans, their attention diverted.

'And not about you and Pierre, either!' she added quietly. 'I was only teasing you.'

Angela nodded.

'I know, but I didn't know he was your Pierre until people told me. And I couldn't have done anything about it if I had known! It was just like a shaft of lightning hitting me. I've never known anything like it.'

Her eyes glowed at the memory.

Florentine smiled ruefully.

'I know. And he wasn't my Pierre, except in my dreams. He has always been his own man, until now.'

And, as she said it, she realised it

didn't hurt any more, well, not much. Neither did she pay any credence to the niggling thoughts she had about her reaction to seeing Charles safe and well. It was simply relief at his safety, wasn't it?

In the following two weeks, Florentine and Angela spent every night out on manoeuvres, working with different operatives each night, getting to know and trust them.

Florentine had thought she knew the salt marshes, but not well enough to satisfy the stringent demands of her compatriots. They had to learn the exact layout of each group of marshes and identify each section by code; how many paces long each bank was and how wide they were; which banks fell away into the deep water or which ones linked with others. They had to draw maps from memory, being accurate on every twist or turn. The information to be learned seemed endless.

'You've just fallen into the sea, Angelique! Try again!'

'You've led your group into a cul-de-sac, Florentine! Bang! Bang! You're dead!'

It was harder for Angela but she gritted her teeth and kept at it, determined to be as accurate as Florentine. They had seen very little of each other since their arrival on the island but they met occasionally for group briefings, and sporadically heard brief mentions of the other. Thoughts of Pierre filled her off-duty times and they met whenever they could, marvelling that they had needed no time to get to know each other before they spoke of their love.

It was as if they had known each other all their lives and had simply been waiting for love to overwhelm them. Both knew it wasn't simply a physical attraction. They were like two halves of one being and times apart were but brief interruptions to be lived through with a longing to be together again.

Angela was staying with a family at La Chevalerie, a small village situated on the edge of the salt marshes just south of Le Chateau, and Florentine was told to make her way there one night as she was to go on a genuine reconnoitre in that area.

As soon as dusk fell, Florentine made her way carefully through the salt marshes to the village of Ors. Every so often, she heard the call of a curlew and she repeated the sound, finding a comfort to know that her compatriots knew where she was. Her route lay through rear gardens, linking pathways created by the residents, but an unfathomable maze to the uninitiated.

She slipped into the shadows of the cottages in La Chevalerie and threaded her way to the one where Angela was staying. They didn't have long to chat to each other but she could tell from Angela's face that she was obviously still very much in love with Pierre.

'I have heard the rumours about him but I know they're not true,' Angela said passionately to Florentine. 'He is very distressed about it but is determined not to let it drive him away. He longs to see his island set free from Germany's yoke. I fear for his safety when he is out, dreading someone coming to tell me he is not coming back!'

Florentine hugged her. 'He is a good operator,' she consoled her, 'and I'm sure he weighs the risks against the outcome. They are all the same. I haven't seen Charles for almost a week and I'm almost afraid to ask if he's all right.' She spoke the words unwittingly, voicing thoughts that lay hidden in the depths of her soul that not even she had been aware of.

'Florentine! You sly thing! Don't tell me you've fallen for him at last.'

Angela looked delighted at the idea, wanting her friend to know the joy that was in her own heart.

'Don't be silly!' Florentine was swift to dispel any such idea. She shrugged her shoulders to emphasise her denial. 'We were friends for so long, I suppose I think of him like a brother.'

Even to herself, her words sounded trite.

'If you say so!' Angela was grinning, totally disbelieving her. Her face sobered again, as her thoughts returned to Pierre and she sighed deeply. 'Pierre volunteers for the most dangerous missions, hoping to prove his true allegiance. He must always be the best, the one who is afraid of nothing!'

Florentine nodded. 'He was the same at school, a real dare-devil! That is why we girls all adored him!'

Angela smiled ruefully, wanting to hold on to that thought.

'I think it is very hard to be in love in wartime.'

Florentine was partly afraid that Angela was becoming depressed by the strain of her concern.

'You mustn't think about it. Concentrate on what you are here for.'

'But we haven't got a transmitter yet! It's so frustrating! We have to keep sending couriers across the island, sending them into unnecessary danger.'

'Don't worry! We'll be getting one soon. Things are happening on the mainland and our liberators are getting closer every day.'

'The sooner the better!'

She looked at Florentine as if undecided whether to say more. Florentine sensed her indecision.

'What is it?'

A slow smile spread over Angela's face. 'We're thinking of getting married.'

Florentine was surprised. 'You've only known him a few weeks!'

'I know . . . but it makes no difference. We know that's what we want. We want to take what happiness we can . . . whilst we can! Who knows what next week might bring?' She excitedly took hold of Florentine's hands.

'Will you be my bridesmaid, Florentine?'

'Of course I will! You know that!' Florentine nodded slowly to herself, acknowledging the depth of love she had seen between them and knowing that she would feel the same way if she were in Angela's position.

They had no time for any more conversation. Angela's co-worker, André, arrived and, soon afterwards, Charles appeared, causing Florentine's heart to skip a beat. She wondered why his lop-sided smile hadn't always affected her in the way it did now. And that curl of his hair that fell over his right eye. Why did she feel the urge to tuck it back into place?

'Where've you been the past few days?' she asked truculently, trying to push her strange thoughts away, hoping Angela hadn't noticed her cheeks turning rosy.

After their earlier conversation, she might misconstrue the cause.

'Missed me, did you?'

'Like toothache!'

'Ouch! Still, I'm back again, and I'm your escort tonight.'

Florentine pulled a face at him, glad that he couldn't read her mind, because she did feel unaccountably pleased. She really had missed him.

'What are we doing?'

'Nothing much,' he said lightly. 'Just checking the marshes for mines and booby-traps.'

'Oh! Well, that's all right, then, isn't it? Angela will be so jealous,' she replied just as lightly.

Charles put his forefinger under her chin and tilted up her face to his. For a shocked moment, Florentine thought he was going to kiss her and couldn't understand why her lips parted slightly and tingled at the thought of his velvet caress.

'Angelique,' he mouthed silently, correcting her slip.

His dark eyes were laughing at her and she had the uncomfortable feeling that he knew that she had been expecting to be kissed.

'Sorry!' she mumbled, dropping her eyes, feeling stupid.

Why did he always have to be the one to notice her mistakes and feel free to correct her? He really was the most insufferable man she knew.

'Shall we go?' she asked coolly. 'I'll see you sometime, Angelique,' she tossed over her shoulder as she stalked through the door.

Charles followed her swiftly.

'Don't take the correction of your mistakes out on Angelique!' he reproved her, misinterpreting the edge to her voice. 'She really is a sweet girl and it's not her fault that you choose to idolise my brother and resent anyone who catches his eye. It's time you grew up, Florentine.'

'And it's time you learned to mind your own business,' she flashed back at him. 'Angelique and I know where we stand!' She wasn't going to tell him that she no longer idolised Pierre! He wouldn't believe her anyway! 'Shall we get on with the job in hand?'

He laid a restraining hand on Florentine's arm. 'This is serious stuff we're doing tonight, Florentine. If you'd rather not do it, tell me now.

We'll be both holding the life of each other in our hands during the next few hours and if that look seemed to say you wished I were dead is really how you feel, then I think I'd better get someone else to work with me.'

'Then I'll just have to pretend that you're Pierre, won't I?' she retaliated crossly. 'And, have no fear, I don't want to besmirch my record by endangering you. I'm a professional, remember.'

'Good. So, with that out of the way, let me brief you on tonight's task. We've had reports that the Germans have been up to something here in the marshes.'

'Why now, all of a sudden? I thought they were concentrating on the northern end by Chassiron and Boyardville.'

'They did, until the Normandy landings. Now, with the Allied Forces spreading out on the mainland, they think, quite rightly in my opinion, that an attack might come from there, which puts St Trojan and the area covered by the salt marshes into the forefront of possible attack. And it won't be long in coming so we've got to be ready. We think they've started placing mines in the marshes, so we need to know exactly where they've put them.'

'And how do we do that?' she asked, as if she didn't know.

'Like I said earlier, we crawl through the marshes until we find them.'

It wasn't quite as random as Charles inferred. The ever-watchful observers had been very precise about the locations where the Germans had been seen to be working, and they reported that the soldiers had returned to their depot at the northern end of the island before nightfall, leaving their insidious weaponry behind them.

Working in pairs, twenty-four local members of the undercover Resistance spent that and succeeding nights making an inch-by-inch search of the terrain, carefully plotting their findings, to be checked by other pairs on subsequent nights.

When Florentine's finger felt the

touch of hard metal, her heart seemed to stop beating. She was crouched down on her knees, her arms stretched out in front of her. Charles was by her side, inching his way forward the same as she was. She took a deep breath and felt again. Her mouth went dry.

'I think I've found something!'

6

'Right! Freeze!' Charles's voice breathed in her ear. Florentine felt his fingers inch their way along her arm until he was at exactly the same position as she was.

'Wriggle back a bit!'

Knowing that Charles had more experience in this sort of warfare, Florentine obeyed without question. This was nothing to do with personalities and differences of opinion. He was the expert and it was strangely warming to know that she could trust his judgement, trust him wholeheartedly, if the truth were told.

She held her breath while Charles carefully followed the outline of the metal shape, confirming Florentine's assessment.

'Good work! Get out your measuring tape. Give me the end, and measure back to the last reference point and write it down. Good. Now, stay where you are. This is a through-lane. I'm going to stride over it and check the other side.'

Florentine's heart was in her mouth as he did as he had said. If the Germans had placed two mines close together, Charles would step on to the second one. She felt a surge of anger at him. Did he have to take that risk? Could he not have played safe and worked his way around to the other side? In the recesses of her mind, she knew that that would have taken too long, and there might have been more mines to check and chart, and more diversions to take. But she felt so frightened for him.

She was startled by the intensity of her fear and, without realising what she was doing, she turned the fear into anger.

There was no explosion. Charles worked his way safely to the next reference point, marked its length and returned to give her a hand as she strode over the mine. He wondered why she was suddenly so brusque with him again and decided that women were a breed apart.

Within two weeks over a hundred mines were located in that area of marshes, with many more in other places, but at least they knew where they were, they hoped.

At the beginning of September the French and Allied Forces arrived on the coast at Rochefort, with only the narrow strip of sea separating them from Île d'Oleron. The mood of the local inhabitants was electrified. Help was at hand.

The euphoric mood was rudely shattered by the escalation of troop activity in the eastern and southern parts of the island. German soldiers were suddenly in every street in Le Chateau and likely to burst into any home or shop at any time. Their grey uniforms were everywhere.

Identity papers were demanded three or four times daily and everyone became more nervy, forever looking over their shoulders to see if anyone was taking an undue interest in what they were saying or to whom they were speaking. Subdued tones and serious faces put their dampener on the small market town.

The first time Florentine's papers were demanded was on a late summer's day as she cycled home from the market one lunch hour. The members of the Resistance had temporarily abandoned their night time activities as being too dangerous and time seemed to drag heavily on Florentine's hands. Charles had been absent for a number of days. Not that she was interested, anyway, she told herself sharply.

Angela had whispered excitedly that Pierre was arranging to have their banns read in church over the next few weeks and that their wedding would be the third Saturday in September. Caught up in the radiant joy that surrounded Angela, Florentine was happily planning which dress she would wear. Her thoughts thus occupied, she pedalled round a corner, straight into a German road-block.

She nearly fell off her bike in shock and barely managed to slam on her brakes, skidding to a standstill a centimetre from the soldier's boots.

'Pardon, monsieur!' she instinctively gasped, in the same manner that she would have apologised to any Frenchman. Her near accident and natural confusion drew some guffaws of laughter from the soldiers manning the roadblock and she had the presence of mind to add her own laughter in a self-deprecating way.

A couple of soldiers called out something she didn't understand and, from the reaction of the one in charge, it must have been something coarse because he sharply reprimanded them. He clicked his heels together and made a stiff bow, nevertheless demanding to see her identity papers.

Thankful for the few moments she had had to collect her thoughts and calm her fast-beating heart, Florentine pulled the required papers out of the bag she wore over her shoulder, praying that they looked as authentic as they needed to be.

The soldier examined them and seemed satisfied. He pointed to her name and said it haltingly in his guttural tones.

Florentine smiled and said, 'Jah,' one of the few German words that she knew, hoping nervously it was the right thing to do.

The soldier said something else. His tone was pleasant and she assumed the words to be complimentary, bringing a faint blush to her cheeks. She cast her eyes down demurely and held out her hand for her papers to be returned to her.

The soldier returned them, clicking his heels together again and making a slight bow of his head as if in salute. She later felt that it was the manner of the incident and her natural reaction that had eased the acceptance of her counterfeit papers. Whatever, she breathed a sigh of relief that her first direct encounter with the enemy had passed successfully.

When her father came home to the bakery an hour or so later, he had a message for her.

'Monsieur Dandonneau says you are to meet Pierre St Clare at La Giraudiere at midnight tonight. A courier is bringing in a radio set tonight and no-one has been able to warn those on the mainland about the mines and the extra activity in the marshes there. He wants you to accompany Pierre to the pick-up point since you know where all the mines are positioned.'

Jacques nodded his head approvingly.

She hugged both her parents and made sure she went to bed early to get some sleep, hardly aware of her change in attitude towards Pierre. He had been the idol of her girlhood, and was now relegated to the past as far as romantic dreams were concerned. She was happy about his impending marriage to Angela. Their love was visible on their faces and in their eyes.

Her mother woke her at ten o'clock. She wanted to allow extra time to cover the couple of miles to La Giraudiere because of the increase of German soldiers in the area. It was as well that she did because she had to make several diversions, sliding down steep banks into the salines; slipping into dark, narrow alleyways; melting into the shadows of outbuildings; even scratching on doors and slipping quickly inside darkened cottages.

She arrived at Madame Naud's cottage before Pierre, and thankfully accepted the hot drink she was offered whilst she waited. She cupped her hands around the mug as she sipped the hot liquid, warming both her hands and the core of her body. She hoped Pierre wasn't much longer. They needed to be at the meeting point before the courier. It was over fifteen minutes later when the quiet scratching at the door warned them that Pierre had arrived, except it wasn't Pierre. It was Philippe.

'Sorry I'm late. I got held up by all the road blocks. Did you? The Germans are all over the place,' he explained as he entered the cottage. 'I should have set off earlier but it was a last-minute change. Pierre has been sent up to Boyardville,' he added. 'Rene Dandonneau thought it best to send me with you, Florentine.'

'Did he? Or was it Charles?' she asked sharply.

'Charles is up north at Chassiron,' Philippe replied, avoiding answering her question directly, she noticed. 'We've had word that there's something going on up there. He has gone to investigate.'

'Hmph! If you say so.' She wasn't totally convinced that it was nothing to do with Charles. How childish could he be? 'I hope you know where all the mines are,' she flung out at Philippe, rattled by the inference behind the change of personnel.

'Well enough!' Philippe retorted. 'We'd better be going, or we'll be late for the rendezvous.'

Pushing aside her personal feelings, Florentine got to her feet. Her body hadn't properly warmed through yet but maybe that was as well. The cold darkness outside wasn't very welcoming and the drier she became, the harder it would be to go back into it.

Soon they were very quickly among the marshes. Twice she had to correct Philippe's choice of path, reminding him of marked positions of mines on the route.

'Let me lead!' she hissed again. 'I've worked this area more than you have!'

'No! Rene appointed me as leader! Hurry up! We are going to be late!'

He was right in that respect. They were late, and Philippe was moving quickly, too quickly in Florentine's opinion.

It wasn't an easy task. Enemy patrols were on the fringe of the area so they didn't dare straighten up. They crouched and crawled, slid down muddy banks and carefully waded in salines known to be safe, though nowhere was one hundred per cent safe.

Suddenly, a faint light shone briefly about two hundred metres ahead. It flickered again, sending the coded call sign.

Florentine heard a low, guttural sound over to their right, perhaps four hundred metres away, taking into consideration how sounds travel far over water, especially at night. She touched Philippe's right arm.

'Germans over there!' she hissed into his ear.

'I know. Stay here. One of us will move faster than two.'

'No, Philippe! Let me go. I know these marshes better than you do. There are two more mines before the open channel. They're both on the main track.'

'I know! Don't worry! I'll miss them.

You stay here,' he repeated.

Against her better judgement, Florentine did as he commanded. He held a superior position to herself and her army training had taught her complete obedience, whether on the field or off it. Reluctantly, she dropped down to the ground and peered worriedly into the darkness ahead, anxiously biting on her lower lip.

Faintly, she heard the German voice again but it didn't seem any nearer and there were no lights coming from that direction. Maybe it was just a patrol on general lookout duty. Hopefully, the patrol would move on before she and Philippe were ready to retrace their steps back to firm ground. How far had he got?

She tried to imagine the route ahead. He would be past the first of the two remaining mines by now. He should be slowing down, approaching the next one carefully. It wasn't in the centre of the path. This one was set towards the left edge. Philippe should be on his hands and knees, his fingers tentatively searching for the tell-tale metal rim of the mine, moving towards its right on the edge of the steep bank down into the marsh.

Everything seemed to happen at once.

A bright light shone straight across the marsh to where the small sailing craft awaited Philippe, lighting up its frail structure.

A harsh command ordered everyone, 'Halte!' A pistol shot rang out, extinguishing the bright light but, in the same instant, a vivid orange light lit the sky ahead.

Florentine saw, or thought she saw, the black silhouette of a man's shape being tossed into the air by the blast and a farther blast that lifted the sailing craft out of the water.

She instinctively dropped back to the ground and covered her head with her arms though none of the flying debris came in her direction.

And then there was silence.

7

Florentine stared blankly, her brain refusing to put into definite thoughts what her eyes had witnessed. She had seen death strike many times during her service in the armed forces, but this was different. This was on her own island, the place where she had spent her childhood.

Philippe had been a year older than she was. He had lived at Dolus and had been around since their teenage years. Now, he was . . .

No! She refused to accept it. He would come crawling back through the marshes and they would marvel at his lucky escape and the others would slap him on the back and say, 'Lucky you!'

But he didn't come.

She didn't know how long she remained frozen. It seemed as though it was a long time but in actual fact was less than a minute. Her training took her over on to automatic pilot and she slid down the steep bank of the saline, her ears alert for sounds of activity from the German soldiers.

There were shouted orders that she didn't understand and the sounds of vehicles moving about on the edge of the marshes. No-one came into the marshes to search for accomplices, though they shone bright searchlights over the area for more than an hour. None picked out her huddled form and eventually all sounds receded and she was left alone to decide what to do, which way to go.

She lay still for over ten minutes after the final sounds had faded away, unconvinced that immediate danger had passed. The Germans might suspect that others were involved and might be waiting for her to make a move. Her clothes were soaked by cold sea-water, her body chilled throughout. She wasn't sure her legs would carry her home but she needed to be setting off to somewhere whilst there was still enough darkness in the sky to hide her.

She tentatively crawled back up the steep slope she had earlier slithered down and listened intently. All she could hear was the gentle lapping of water away in the distance where the marshes met the sea. It drew her gaze and she stared in the direction of where she had seen the violent explosion. Was it possible that Philippe had survived? That he had only been injured? What about the courier? The sailing craft? The rest of the crew? Surely at least one had survived! And their much-needed transmitter! It couldn't be lost! They needed it so badly! She made the plaintive noise of the curlew and waited expectantly, hopefully, but only silence greeted her listening ears. Although emotionally she refused to accept that all were dead, her professional mind knew that to try to verify the fact would be putting herself into needless danger.

There was nothing she could do. Even if the transmitter had survived the blast, it could have been blown anywhere. There would be a small enough chance of finding it in daylight — none at all in the darkness and fast-approaching half light. No, she had to get away from the scene and let others decide if the chance of finding the transmitter undamaged at a future date might be worth the risk of danger.

She didn't want to risk incriminating Madame Naud by returning there, besides which, it was out of the way to go back there. Neither did she want to make her way to the cottage where Angela was living. If the Germans were to search any dwelling places, those of La Giraudiere and La Chevalerie would be the nearest ones and therefore their obvious targets. She had either to make her way home and risk being caught outside during the hours of curfew, or stay out in the marshes until morning and hope to get a lift on a farm vehicle going to the market.

It was the latter course of action that she chose. There were many isolated wooden cabins scattered about the marshes.

She wasn't really conscious of counting her steps, making the right choices through the maze of pathways through the marshes but she eventually arrived at the wooden huts on the bank of Chenal d'Ors on the north-eastern side of the marshes, their silhouettes standing out against the lightening sky. She was cold and weary and was finding it difficult to think properly.

The sound of a curlew drifted softly through the air, penetrating her numbed mind. Of course! People had heard the explosions. They knew something was amiss and were on the look-out for survivors. She shrank into the shadows and repeated the sound. An answer came from her right and she echoed it again softly.

Two dark-clad figures closed in on her and asked for her code-word. On her response, one whispered, 'This way!' and she followed them through the lines of huts until they halted outside of one of them and, after tapping a series of tiny raps on the glass window, the door opened slightly and she was ushered inside. The small hut seemed to be full of men but in reality there were only three others beside themselves.

A small storm lantern provided a flickering glow and she recognised Raoul Dandonneau, the network leader of the group based at Ors. He bade her be seated and one of the men draped a rough blanket around her shoulders, though it didn't stop her teeth chattering and her limbs shaking, as much as in the aftermath of shock as from the cold.

'Tell us what happened, Florentine,' Raoul demanded softly.

Haltingly, she recounted the events of the evening, eventually dropping her face into her hands and sobbing, 'He's dead! Philippe's dead! And the courier and the others on the boat! They're all dead, and we still haven't got a transmitter! They have died for nothing!'

One of the men laid a hand on her shoulder.

'Not for nothing. They died for the liberation of Île d'Oleron. Many more of us may die, but we will be liberated one day soon.'

It was little consolation to her at that moment. She felt guilty to have survived when others had died. Was there anything she should have done differently? She knew the marshes better than Philippe. Should she have insisted on being the one to lead and not taken his refusals so readily?

One of the men put a drink of brandy in her hands and she sipped tentatively at the fiery liquid. It rasped the back of her throat and nearly made her choke but its warmth soon began to spread around her body.

When she awoke, streaks of light were glimmering through the edges of the black cloth that covered each window. Three of the men still remained and she could hear their low voices still discussing the night's events. She heard one of the men talk of betrayal and toss the name of Pierre St Clare into the frame, provoking an immediate argument between the other two.

'No! No, he didn't!' Florentine protested, struggling to sit up. 'He was to have been my partner until the last moment. He wouldn't betray me. He wouldn't betray anyone. Pierre isn't like that.'

'Who is like that?' Raoul asked quietly. 'Does a traitor look any different than his compatriots?'

'But he wouldn't betray the operation when he was to be part of it. Not even if he weren't,' Florentine insisted. He just wouldn't! She knew it.

The sound of a cart being driven along the track outside brought their argument to a sudden close. They were instantly alert to possible danger. One of the men flattened himself against the wall near to a window and he carefully eased the black-covering away from the glass so that he could peer out through the opening he had made without being seen himself.

'It's Charles St Clare!' he said quietly. 'Let him in.'

Charles slipped through the narrowly-opened door and strode straight over to Florentine.

'Florentine! You're safe! I got such a garbled message, I wasn't sure.'

Florentine rose to greet him thankfully, holding out her hands to him.

'Charles! Oh, I'm so glad to see you. Tell them it was nothing to do with Pierre. He hadn't betrayed the operation. Tell them!'

Charles had taken hold of her hands, as if he were about to pull her to him in an embrace but, at her words, he jerked his head around to fix his gaze on Raoul and Nicolas, the other man.

Raoul shrugged.

'It's a question we have to ask ourselves,' he said quietly. 'How is it the Germans were there at exactly the right time? Was it purely by chance or had they had a tip-off? It's not the first time your brother has been connected with an operation that has gone wrong.'

'No, and he's not the only one. I knew about it. Do you suspect me? Victor knew about it and so did Denis and Paul. Are they under suspicion, too?'

Raoul met Charles's gaze calmly but his eyes were icy cold.

'That is the insidious nature of any betrayal — we are all under suspicion, every one of us who knew about it! But Pierre has been under suspicion before. How many coincidences do we need before we take action?'

'But Pierre was supposed to be part of the operation!' Florentine burst in. 'He wouldn't put himself into danger, would he? He isn't stupid.'

'No, he isn't stupid, mademoiselle. He might have expected the last-minute change,' Nicolas suggested. 'Or maybe he was planning to drop out at the last moment. Who knows? Why exactly was the change made? And under whose authority?' The question was directed at Charles.

Florentine turned swiftly and looked at Charles, trying to will him to take the spotlight away from Pierre. Pierre wasn't the traitor.

Her heart began to sink heavily. She could detect an unwillingness in Charles to speak. He would be wanting to protect her reputation, she guessed, and not wanting to implicate her in his decision, but issues far more important than her reputation were at stake. Pierre's honour was in question, maybe, even his life.

Florentine cast down her eyes.

'It was my fault,' she admitted quietly, drawing the attention back to herself, away from Charles's obvious reluctance to tell the truth and implicate his brother. 'Charles knows that I have always idolised Pierre, imagined myself in love with him, even. And now he is engaged to be married to my best friend.' She raised her head

115

again, her eyes sorrowful. 'Charles obviously feared that I would use the occasion to flirt with Pierre, and, perhaps, endanger the operation.'

'And would you have done so?' Raoul asked sharply.

Florentine thought quickly. She knew that she wouldn't have done so. She was no longer idealistically captivated by the hero of her teenage years, but if she admitted such, it would possibly weaken Charles's motive in removing him from the operation.

'I do not know. I think I would have acted professionally. I hope so! But, I do not know.' She stared miserably at the ground, hating to let Charles go on thinking that she still cared for Pierre in a romantic fashion but she knew that was why he had acted as he had.

'Is that so, Charles?' Raoul asked.

Florentine flickered her gaze at Charles, willing him to agree in order to give Pierre the best benefit of the doubt. Charles glanced at her coolly.

'It might have been the case, if the decision had been mine — but it wasn't. René Cailloleau made the decision to send Pierre to Boyardville instead of on this operation. You will have to ask him what his reason was. All I know is that it was at the very last minute and Pierre set off to Boyardville immediately. He would have had no time to pass on any information to the enemy, nor to anyone else.'

Florentine listened in dismay. She felt herself washed by mixed emotions, Relief that Pierre truly had been diverted for a genuine reason, and dismay that she had let Charles think that she was still enamoured by his brother. He was looking at her in derision and it suddenly mattered to her very much that he didn't think badly of her.

She would have to tell Charles of her changed feelings towards Pierre as soon as they were on their way back to Le Chateau. She would tell him of Pierre's and Angela's wedding plans and that she was going to be Angela's bridesmaid.

Satisfied that she would be able to sort things out satisfactorily, she smiled disarmingly at Raoul Dandonneau.

'I knew Pierre would not have betrayed us,' she said. 'I think he would prefer to die rather than be dishonoured.'

'The men who died tonight did not have the choice, Mademoiselle Devreux. Whether or not tonight's tragedy was the result of betrayal, I fear we have a traitor in our midst and I would urge you not to treat my words lightly. I have personally known every member of our island's Resistance movement for many years and I wish I could say amen to your naïve judgment. Unfortunately, most men have a price — even an honourable price. Just pray that you are never called upon to declare yours.'

'An honourable price?' Florentine queried. 'How can the price of betrayal ever be called honourable?'

Raoul regarded her puzzled face sympathetically.

'If a man's family is held to ransom for the price of betrayal, who does the man betray? His family or his comrades? Either way, he has betrayed. Who is to say which is the more dishonourable? A man must make his own decisions and live with the consequences, if he can. But we must still identify that man and remove him from our midst. Otherwise, we can trust no-one, and our work will cease to be effective.

'We have sworn to lay aside personal affections and strive for the liberation of our island. Do not allow yourself to be drawn away from that goal, mademoiselle, unless you wish to resign right now.'

Florentine listened in silence, sensing a rebuke couched within his words. She nodded slowly, accepting the censure. He was right. Whom would Pierre choose, his comrades or Angela?

She was conscious of Charles standing at her side, thankful that he couldn't read her thoughts — saddened, for now he despised her, and with good cause.

She had carelessly spurned his love and chased after something that wasn't real.

For a moment, hope burned within her that she could declare her realisation of where her heart lay, but she quenched it at its birth. It was better that he didn't know, or maybe he would be tempted to betray his comrades for her if the occasion arose. He would fight with a clearer mind without the knowledge of her love, and so would she.

She raised her eyes and looked at Raoul.

'You are right, monsieur, I am sorry. The liberation of the island comes before everything, even those we love. I will indeed pray that I make the right decision if I ever have to choose.'

'Good! Nicolas will escort you home. Try to have a good sleep. We may need you again tonight. Charles, stay here and make your report about what is going on at Chassiron.'

Florentine quietly said her farewell. She needed time to sort out her newly-discovered feelings for Charles and was relieved that she could postpone her next time alone with him.

8

Charles watched Florentine leave with mixed emotions. His relief at finding her unharmed was now soured by her unashamed confession that she might have been tempted to flutter her eyes at his brother. How could she be so brazen as to admit her feelings so openly?

Why did he keep hoping she would forget Pierre and turn to him? It obviously wasn't going to happen and the sooner he accepted that fact, the better it would be.

Pushing thoughts of Florentine to the far reaches of his mind, he passed on to his area leader all the information he had discovered. The Germans had drafted in a large number of troops from other areas and were amassing at St Denis and the outlying hamlets at the northerly end of the island near

Chassiron and Domino.

They were also requisitioning a number of farm carts. Were they expecting an Allied attack in that area in the near future?

'If only the Allied troops on the mainland could let us know what is happening out there!' Charles burst out bitterly, his own inner torment adding vehemence to his words. 'We needed that transmitter.'

Raoul shook his head.

'I don't think there's to be an Atlantic attack, not now that the Allies have reached Rochefort on the mainland, unless it's a move to split the Germans' attention.' He stroked his chin thoughtfully.

'The Allies might be trying to create a diversion. You're right. We need to know exactly what is happening up there.'

He thumped his clenched fist against the wall in frustration.

'I'll get straight back there,' Charles volunteered. It was just what he needed

to take him away from Florentine
. . . an operation at the other end of the
island. 'I'll take a cart-load of salt to
the fishermen at St Denis. That will get
me right in the middle of the action.'

Raoul nodded in agreement.

'Good. Whom will you take with you?
You need someone fleet of foot who
might be able to return to us more
quickly than you could manage with
your wagon and oxen.'

Charles considered some options.

'There's Michel or Georges. No,
they're too well-known. How about
Raymond? He's not been seen around
much.'

'A woman would be better, less
conspicuous than two men together
and not posing as great a threat. Take
Mademoiselle Devreux. It will do her
good to get away from here for a few
days, give her a change of scene. And
she's proving to be one of our best
undercover agents.'

Charles's heart sank. Florentine was
the last person he wanted to work with

closely on a mission that might take two or three days.

'She needs to get some sleep,' he objected.

'We all need sleep, and we all suffer flashbacks,' Raoul snapped. 'She can sleep in the back of your wagon.' His face softened. 'You are old friends. You will be good for each other. You will be able to comfort her about Philippe.' His expression resumed his usual briskness. 'Load up your wagon. I'll get word to Mademoiselle Devreux to be at your farm by mid-morning. You should make it to St Denis before curfew. If not, stable your wagon and animal somewhere and continue on foot, and get word back as soon as you can. We need to know what they're doing.'

Florentine felt her heart leap in joyful anticipation when the message came from Raoul that she was to accompany Charles to Chassiron.

Dressed in old clothes, with her face and arms smeared with dust and her hair dulled with grease and dust in an effort to dim her attractiveness, she cycled towards the Dolus gateway that led out of town. She was stopped at the barrier and had to show her papers. It was a keen-eyed young officer who scrutinised her work permit.

'Where are you going?' he demanded curtly, his eyes flickering over her.

'To work on the farm,' she said flatly, keeping her eyes cast down, hoping the work permit looked genuine enough to satisfy his inspection.

Her heart beat rapidly as the officer paused to consider the permit. The failure of the previous night's mission weighted heavily upon her, knocking her confidence. She had hardly recognised her white-faced, red-eyed reflection in her bedroom mirror when she had arrived home this morning. Philippe's face continually loomed before her as if in reproof, but she knew she had done her best to persuade him to let her go ahead. It didn't help her to accept his death, however, nor that of the boat crew and the loss of the precious transmitter.

It was so frustrating not to be able to do the job she and Angela had been sent over to do! They should have been allowed to carry their own transmitter set!

Was last night's failed operation the reason why the German officer was taking his time? She was always nervous at roadblocks but had learned not to let it show. The Germans seemed to be tightening up on security. Was their mission to Chassiron connected in some way, she wondered.

A covered wagon entering the town drew the officer's attention and he abruptly returned her permit and, to her great relief, waved her through. She turned towards the inner coast road, following the edge of the low sand dunes and the gently-lapping water of the narrow channel between the island and the mainland.

The lane that led to Domaine St Clare, where Charles's and Pierre's family had lived for past generations, was just ahead and she turned into it. She hid her bicycle in a ditch close to the farm entrance and went into the farmyard.

Charles was harnessing an ox to a wagon when she arrived. Her heart filled with longing at the sight of him. He was wearing serge trousers and a checked shirt that was open at the neck and with rolled-up sleeves, showing his tanned skin. His body was lean and strong.

Florentine's mouth felt dry. How lightly she had spurned his embraces. She remembered the kiss they had shared on the beach only a few weeks ago and her lips tingled as she longed to repeat the experience. Should she at least explain why she had let Raoul think she still had fond feelings for Pierre? She moved towards him, her face betraying her indecision.

'Charles, I want to explain . . . '

'I think you've said enough, Florentine,' he said curtly to her. 'I don't think it would be wise to say any more, do you?'

His face looked devoid of emotion as he continued, 'You weren't my first choice for my partner on this mission but Raoul seems to have great faith in you.'

He turned away to pick up his jacket that was laid across the hitching rail.

'You are here in a professional capacity only, and that's how I want it to remain. Is that understood?'

His words almost broke her heart. Florentine swallowed hard. She tightened her lips. If that was how he wanted to play it then it was fine by her. There was no way she was going to beg or plead for forgiveness.

'The same goes for me,' she said lightly, fighting the despair that flowed through her. 'I wouldn't have chosen to come with you but Raoul seemed to think I should get away from . . . ' It was almost too much to say. ' . . . from last night.' She turned away so that he wouldn't see the tears that threatened to spill from her eyes.

Did he think she should have used her intimate knowledge of the area better and prevented the accident? The vivid orange light flashed across her memory, and the black silhouette of Philippe as he was flung spread-eagled into the air.

Her features twisted in agony and she was glad Charles couldn't see her face at that moment.

'The wagon is ready. You had better get aboard,' she heard Charles say.

Her moment of terror passed as she took a grip on herself and she was able to clamber aboard the wagon and sit on the wooden driving seat.

After that, it wasn't very hard for her to keep to her decision to remain aloof from Charles, and Charles treated her with decided coolness as he sat stiffly beside her.

They travelled in silence for a few miles. Never had Florentine felt so ill at ease in his company. Eventually, to break the unnatural silence between them, she told him of Angela's and Pierre's plans to marry in three weeks time, keeping her voice carefully neutral. She wished she could convince him how pleased she was but knew he wouldn't believe her.

She had never been under any illusions about Pierre's feelings towards her. Until he met Angela, Pierre had never loved anyone but himself. But Charles was a naturally warm-hearted person. She had taken his affection for her for granted, until she had lost it, she reflected bitterly.

'Can't we at least be friends?' she asked Charles eventually, hurt beyond measure by his disdain of her.

'I hope I will always be your friend, Florentine,' he replied quietly, barely taking his eyes from the track ahead, 'but I think the less we see of each other the better it will be for both of us, apart from when we are assigned on missions together, when I hope we are both professional enough to put our personal feelings aside.'

Florentine couldn't bear to see the bleakness in his eyes and was glad that his glance towards her had been brief. She, too, stared ahead, though she saw nothing.

Keeping to lesser-used tracks to avoid the roadblocks set between the principal villages, they plodded steadily in a north-westerly direction. How different it might have been if she hadn't spurned his love for so long, she reflected sadly. She imagined snuggling close to him, her head on his shoulder. With her arms around him, she would feel the beating of his heart and smell the masculine fragrance of him.

They skirted east of St Pierre, following the edge of the salines to Sauzelle, and then travelling west of St Georges to Chaucre and finally to the small port of St Denis. Dusk was fast approaching but several other wagons were on the road, blatantly ignoring the fast-approaching hour of curfew. The surly expressions of their French drivers showed that they were unwilling participants in whatever task they were doing. The presence of a German soldier on most of the wagons prevented the hope of any conversation between the conscripted drivers.

'What's happening?' Florentine whispered to Charles.

'I'm not sure. Wagons were being seized from local farms yesterday but I had no way of discovering what's happening because there was a German soldier riding on each wagon. Tonight, I intend to find out!'

Charles jostled his wagon into line, nodding briefly to the other drivers. Florentine wasn't sure but she felt she detected a glimmer in their eyes as if they knew who he was.

'There's a roadblock ahead,' Florentine warned in alarm.

Her mouth went dry. Would they accept they were making a delivery?

Charles assumed a bland expression on his face. When they reached the head of the queue, he pulled back on the rein, halting the wagon.

The German soldiers stepped forward.

'Your pass?' one demanded.

Charles handed the man his travel pass, grinning inanely.

'I've got sacks of salt for the fishermen of St Denis, but soldiers said to come here. We do as they say. Can we go now?' His simple amiability seemed to deflect any suspicious notions the officer might have had.

'Not yet. Who's your passenger?'

Charles grinned.

'She's my sister. She looks after me. She's bossy. You like her?'

Florentine scowled at the soldier, glad that she had made herself look extremely undesirable.

The soldier made a derisory comment and laughed coarsely at his companion. Florentine didn't need to understand German to know that she had been rejected.

The soldier stepped back a pace.

'Dump your load and then follow

the others,' he commanded, nodding to the next soldier in line. The soldier leaped on to the wagon and Charles flicked the reins, guiding his ox out of line.

He handed the reins to Florentine.

'Hold him steady, Florrie!'

He jumped down and ambled to the rear of the wagon where the soldier was already stacking the sacks near the tail-end.

Florentine seethed indignantly. Florrie, indeed!

She could hear Charles grumbling about what his boss would do to him when he returned with no money for his load of salt but the soldier paid no attention.

'Just do as you're told!' he ordered.

When their wagon was empty, the soldier grasped Florentine's shoulder roughly and pushed her towards the rear of the cart. His harsh words and jerk of his head told Florentine that she was to give up her seat to him and ride in the back of the wagon.

'Get back into line!' he then ordered Charles.

Wagons were being sent in different directions. Charles was directed to follow two others and they lumbered their way slowly towards the rocky headland at the most northerly part of the island where the tall black and white lighthouse had stood for many years, shining its light seaward.

A couple of large, concrete look-out bunkers stood starkly on the cliff-top at the side of the lighthouse, their squat silhouettes just visible against the dark night sky. The lighthouse beamed no guiding light to warn mariners of the out-jutting rocks at its base. They would approach at their own peril.

The shadowy figures of German soldiers were waiting for the conscripted farm vehicles. Charles and Florentine were ordered down and commanded to help to load heavy gun equipment on to their wagon. Florentine did her best to comply. Charles bore most of the weight and they managed to lift the heavy pieces of iron canons on to the wagon.

'And this one?' Florentine asked, putting her hand on another canon.

'No!'

The refusal was sharp and Florentine jumped away. Her touch had been brief but it was long enough to detect a difference in material. The one left behind was made of wood. A moment's pondering gave her the reason. It was a wooden replica canon. She nodded slightly in appreciation of the ploy. It would be put with others of its kind in the now-empty positions of the genuine canons that had been removed. To anyone too far away to determine what the canons were made of, they would appear to be genuine weapons and, perhaps, deter an assault.

She bit her lip in frustration. Without a radio transmitter they couldn't let the Allies know of the deception. She tucked the information away in the back of her mind and concentrated on the task in hand. They were heading back towards the south of the island, taking heavy weaponry with them.

It was a long journey back. The ox was tired and its load heavy. Florentine could sense Charles's anger when the soldier snatched his whip and lashed the animal's back. She tried to stay awake, hoping to be able to work out their possible destination but the previous night's activities took their toll on her and eventually her heavy eye-lids closed in sleep.

It took her a few seconds on awaking to remember where she was. Her whole body ached and she was cold and sore. The sky above her had paled and a low mist hovered over the ground. She raised herself painfully on to her elbows and looked over the rim of the wagon sides. It was difficult to orientate herself. There were so few distinctive places in the country lanes in the middle of the island. Where were they?

The sun hadn't risen but she detected the glimmer of dawn slightly left. So they were travelling east southeast, somewhere on the inland coast.

She stretched her limbs and made her voice sound sleepy, drawing out the first word as if it were a waking sound.

'Ou sont-nous? Where are we?'

Charles didn't reply straight away and Florentine wondered if he hadn't heard. But then he flicked his whip and sucked in his cheeks making a clicking sound to encourage the tired ox.

'Arceau!'

Florentine smiled. Arceau was a small village north of Dolus and, across the salines, on the coast, was the Point of Arceau where a deep, narrow channel flowed into the marshes. That would be a possible place for the Allies to make an assault on the island and an ideal place for the Germans to position a canon!

Soon afterwards, Charles repeated the encouraging clicking sound, followed by the single word, 'Va!'

He was telling her to go!

The soldier's shoulders were hunched

and Florentine guessed he was barely awake. She edged her way slowly to the end of the wagon. They were approaching a crossroad on the unmetalled track. It was unmanned.

Florentine glanced over her shoulder. The soldier was unaware of her movements. She gathered her skirt high up her thighs and clambered on to the tailgate. Holding her breath, she waited until Charles slowed the pace of the wagon and dropped to the ground.

She rolled as she fell, softening the blow as she landed on the hard earth and then immediately rolled over and over into the tall grasses that bordered the track. She stopped rolling and lay still, waiting for the harsh, guttural sound that would herald the soldier's observance of her departure, but it didn't come.

Florentine picked herself up, brushed down her skirt and set off at a loping run towards Le Chateau.

A glimmer of expectation rose in her heart. The Germans were moving their defences to the inland coast. A liberating attack from the Allied armies must be expected.

The end was in sight!

But where would that leave her and Charles? Could she bear to let him walk out of her life after only so recently discovering that it was him whom she loved?

From the coolness he had displayed towards her in the past few days, it seemed as though she wouldn't have any choice in the matter.

9

The news was welcomed by the local leaders. Something had alarmed the occupying army and they were making defensive manoeuvres. They were on the run.

But, if the end was indeed in sight, it wasn't immediately noticeable.

The islanders watched helplessly as a great number of fortifications were swiftly constructed in the southern part of the island, each position protected by mines and barbed wire and a network of trenches with places to fire the artillery, making local attempts at sabotage well-nigh impossible.

The German Commandant took possession of the citadel and reinforced its fortifications, increasing the menacing presence of the occupying troops. The sharp sound of marching jackboots became commonplace in the small town and the islanders learned to live with the surge of fear they felt when a sudden banging on the door of their house heralded yet another house-search.

Like the rest of the would-be saboteurs, Charles fumed and fretted at their restricted movements and their utter helplessness. Florentine rarely saw him and, although she felt bereft without him, she knew he wasn't yet ready to forgive what he saw as her willingness to betray her friend. She had better try to forget him and learn to live her life without him.

But her heart wouldn't obey her head. She yearned for him with an inconsolable longing.

Her undercover work was the only solace to her heartache. Sent out to monitor the beaches, Florentine and her comrades identified anti-landing defences covering eight kilometres of the island's beaches. She feared there would be nowhere left for the Allies to be able to make a successful landing when the right time came.

They tried to shut their ears to the constant sound of sawing and hammering that was heard in the forest of St Trojan as the pines were sawn down to make booby-traps to slow down the progress of enemy troops. And undercover watchers feared that many of the plethora of newly-scattered mines in the salt marshes were undetected by them. The island was like a powder keg with a short fuse.

Some of the local French freedom fighters were just as determined to keep the upper hand. As Florentine was about to leave a secret meeting in the cellar at Domaine St Clare she overheard a snatch of muted conversation.

'There was more activity around Arceau last night,' she heard in quiet undertones. 'I need to check it out tonight. How are you fixed for coming with me?'

Florentine stopped in her tracks. No-one was foolhardy enough to venture into the marshes at the moment, surely. It was far too danger-ous. Their charts were well out-of-date.

Even before she turned she knew who had spoken. Before Andre could make his reply, she pushed between him and Charles.

'Did I hear you right?' she hissed angrily. 'Do you think you are invincible that you can continue to spy out the salines in spite of Rene's decision to cancel other operations?' she demanded.

Her throat hurt as she spoke, her fear for his safety was so great. How could he be so reckless? Didn't he care if he was killed?

Charles faced her, his face outwardly calm.

'Someone has to go, Florentine.' He raised an eyebrow, giving him a slightly cynical expression. 'Who better than someone who has no dependents? We have to keep the salines open. That is where our liberators will come.'

She knew he was right, but why him? She wanted to scream at him that she depended on him to stay alive, that she would not want to continue to live if he were taken out of her life. Her thoughts were so strong that she wondered if she had actually screamed the words . . . but she hadn't.

Charles regarded her coolly.

'Believe me, Florentine, I have every intention of being here when the island is liberated,' he added, his voice lighter than the gleam in his eyes indicated. 'I keep a cool head because I allow nothing to distract me, unlike such as my brother, who is so readily distracted these days.'

Florentine narrowed her eyes at his criticism of Pierre and searched his face for hidden meaning. Was he implying that he thought she was still trying to attract Pierre?

'And what are you suggesting?' she asked coldly. 'It isn't me who is distracting Pierre, I can assure you.'

'Good! Then let's keep it that way, shall we?'

Florentine reflected how closely tied

were the emotions of hatred and love. At that moment, she felt she hated Charles. She pressed her lips together and, swinging away from him, blindly hurried up the steps away from him, her head erect and her back ramrod straight. There was no way she was going to let him know how much his attitude towards her hurt.

Two days later, Florentine's father, Jacques Devreux, was lying on the roof of his family home, his binoculars trained on the neighbouring mainland, when he spotted regular flashes of light beaming across the narrow channel.

'Florentine! Get up here immediately!' he called down through the skylight, nearly slipping down the roof in his excitement.

'What is it, Papa?'

Her breath was ragged after running up the attic steps.

'Out there! See! That flashing light! What does it say?'

'Quick! A piece of paper . . . Oh! Don't stop! Don't stop!'

The messenger didn't stop. He or she continued to flash the coded message throughout the afternoon. The first of the Allied Forces had arrived on the mainland coast opposite Île d'Oleron. It was the 9th September, 1944. On that day, the Battalion Roland, under Rene Tallet, occupied the nearby towns of Marennes, Hiers and Brouage.

The islanders were jubilant as they watched the Germans evacuating their tenuous mainland position and taking refuge in Fort Louvois, a small, fortified tower on a rocky mass in the shallow waters between the mainland and the island. That evening, Captain Lucien Leclerc and his men occupied the tiny town of Bourcefranc, facing their goal across two kilometres of water. Captain Leclerc made contact with the German Commander on Île d'Oleron but the ultimatum he gave was rejected. The Germans had no intention of abandoning the island yet.

Florentine was under orders to keep constant watch on the mainland from their rooftop. Various others came to relieve her. She found herself both hoping that Charles would be one of them and dreading the same the very next moment.

Neither her hopes nor her fears were realised. He did not come.

Two days later, early in the morning, six enemy boats came from La Rochelle, attempting to land at Bourcefranc but were repulsed by the Allied armies on the mainland. Florentine and her companions were jubilant, until the Germans taking refuge in Fort Louvois evacuated the fort and retreated by boats to Île d'Oleron, adding their number to the occupation army.

Florentine's patience in watching out for another message was finally rewarded by a series of signals from Captain Leclerc. The leaders of the island's Resistance were swiftly summoned to the small attic room above the bakery to discuss Leclerc's messages. They no longer felt alone. Their countrymen were in sight across the narrow stretch of water, but under constant bombardment from the canons now set up along the inland coast of the island and from the fortified citadel.

That was hard for the islanders to bear. Shellfire from French soil was killing French citizens.

The ceaseless sound of assault was deafening as the two armies tried to bring each other into submission. The Germans were determined to hold on as long as they could.

The islanders, fearful of recriminations and retaliations, tried to live inconspicuously, both hopeful and fearful at the same time, knowing that the liberating barrage of warfare could kill or maim them, as well as the Germans soldiers.

Underneath their cowed appearance, they were awaiting the promised command to act.

Two weeks of bombardment passed.

Pierre and Angela, determined not to let the intensified warfare prevent their marriage, made their vows to each other in the packed church of Le Chateau on the third Saturday in September. Angela looked radiant and Florentine beamed her delighted pleasure as Angela handed her bouquet to her in order to enable Pierre to place the ring upon her finger.

Florentine was aware that Charles was looking at her, his face slightly puckered in perplexity. She studiously refused to meet his eyes. Let him think what he wished. It was no longer any concern of his what she felt or thought.

So, why did her heart suddenly beat a little faster? Did she hope he might at last discern the truth? She sighed sadly, glad that Charles's eyes had returned to face the priest. She glanced at his profile surreptitiously.

His expression was strangely gentle as he listened to the familiar words the priest was saying to the newly-married couple and Florentine's heart leaped again. If only he would look at her like that!

There was no honeymoon for the newly-weds. Angela joined the rest of the St Clare family at the farm. Whenever Florentine saw her, she looked blissfully happy, and there was a tenderness in Pierre that was new to his nature.

One afternoon in late September, Florentine received orders to make her way to Domaine St Clare. Charles was detailed to lead a welcome party to the Arceau Channel, hopefully to greet a group of ten would-be liberators and lead them to places of safety somewhere on the island to await further instructions.

Charles knew exactly where the canon and other artillery had been placed, though it was all well guarded and all access to the inner coast had been cut off.

Sixteen Resistance members met at the farm that night, all quietly composed and ready for action.

Charles briskly divided them into two groups, one group to put the canon and other artillery out of action and the second group to each lead a liberator to a specific hiding place.

Charles put himself in the first group with five other men.

Florentine had expected no less. It irked her feminine pride to be in the second group but her honest self-assessment agreed with the decision. She hadn't done any hand-to-hand fighting and wasn't sure how she would react if she had to attempt to kill an enemy soldier. She tried not to think of what Charles's group might have to face.

Her heart beat rapidly when the two groups split up. What if Charles was killed? How would she cope? She wanted to run after him and tell him that she loved him, but she knew it was a foolish notion. He needed to be cool-headed and dispassionate, and, besides, she wasn't sure her love was shared.

It seemed a long wait. No sounds came from where they knew the canon to be positioned. Had the assault failed? The ten men and women were tense as they waited in silence, their bodies cold and cramped.

The plaintive cry of the curlew pierced the night air, stabbing their hearts with joy. Andre, their appointed group leader, responded with the same call and a straggled line of men dressed in black clothes and with blackened faces crept towards them. Each carried a bundle wrapped in oilskins. How Florentine hoped that there was a radio transmitter and receiver amongst them.

Their two leaders made themselves known to each other and divided the newly-arrived men between the waiting guides.

Florentine hoped to see Charles before she left, but that wasn't to be. A lean, dark figure was assigned into her care and she signalled wordlessly to him to follow her through the maze of the salines. It took them five hours to make their way stealthily to Grand Gibou on the western side of Le Chateau, a distance of about eight or nine miles. There were a number of close shaves, when enemy patrols were almost encountered but the noise of their vehicles warned of their coming and Florentine and her companion were able to slide into cover long before the vehicles were upon them.

Nonetheless, it was a scary journey and Florentine was relieved when they reached their destination and she handed her man over to the next contact. He, in turn, would take him somewhere else and only the last contact would know of his whereabouts.

The sky was getting lighter. Florentine lay concealed until the first farm vehicle approached her position and slowed its pace, allowing her to climb aboard. She slipped back into the town without being apprehended.

Within a few days, word passed around that a man called Pierre Joguet and sergeant-in-chief, Jean Boussac, were in control of the new group and that they had smuggled in with them a small amount of arms and explosives and were under orders to reorganise the Oleronais Resistance.

To Florentine's intense disappointment, there was still no transmitter on the island. Nevertheless, with the increased number of trained men dispersed throughout the island, they were able to collect more information about enemy activities and pass the information on to other groups by courier.

It was over a week later before any moves were made to bring the various groups together to make plans for a concerted assault upon the German positions. Messages were passed back and forth; the armaments and explosives were distributed among a number of central holding positions; and everyone was keyed up for the night-time assault at the end of the second week of October.

Their dreams were shattered on the tenth of October.

Most people were asleep when the German jeeps screeched to a stop outside chosen dwelling places throughout the island. The clatter of soldiers' boots rang out across the cobbled streets, followed by heavy bangs upon the doors. Householders who didn't open their doors quickly enough to satisfy the soldiers' impatience, found themselves facing a splintered door and were put under immediate arrest while soldiers ransacked every room, attic and cellar.

Most of the smuggled armaments and explosives were found and confiscated. All people found within the houses containing explosives were arrested and taken away for questioning and certain imprisonment.

At Boyardville, the sergeant-in-chief, Jean Boussac, Sergeant Andre Gerent and Reni Nomme were discovered and later interred in the citadel at La Chateau. Of these, Jean Boussac was condemned to death. The others were imprisoned.

The Oleronais Resistance and the morale of the island as a whole were shattered by the act. How did the Germans know which houses or other buildings to search?

The answer was obvious . . .

Once again they had been betrayed by a traitor in their midst.

An uneasy atmosphere of suspicion fell upon all active members who were in any way involved in the planning or carrying out of orders. Once again, names were bandied about as everyone sought to discover the culprit. As before, suspicion fell on the inner band of local leaders. Pierre and Andre were still on the list, but this time, another name was added.

Charles St Clare was also under suspicion.

10

'How can you begin to even think it is true?' Florentine demanded of her father. 'You know that Charles has taken more risks than any of us! Without him, I doubt the Resistance would have survived this long. It's insane to think he might be the traitor.'

'Maybe his risks weren't all that risky,' Jacques suggested. 'He has had some remarkably lucky escapes, you must admit.'

'So what!' Florentine demanded, speaking with unaccustomed vehemence to her father. 'He is a good undercover agent, and he has been lucky, like many others of us.'

Jacques placed his hands on his daughter's shoulders, looking sadly into her eyes.

'War makes many demands on a man,' he said. 'No-one is immune.'

A few weeks dragged by. Either no-one seemed to know anything about Charles's whereabouts, or no-one was saying, and Florentine could only hope that no news simply meant that he was on an undercover mission somewhere.

The warmth of the summer faded away and autumn seemed to make an all-too-brief appearance that year. The nights were long, dark and cold, ideal conditions for undercover work. The members of the local Resistance who were still able to do active service made excellent use of the opportunity, once again building up a network of information.

Jean Boussac, who had been arrested and condemned to death in October, managed to escape from the citadel, giving hope to the families of other prisoners who were still held there. His escape heralded a spate of undercover sabotage activities to harass the enemy.

Many quietly believed that they had the enemy on the run, which made it all the more a blow when Florentine arrived home from active duties early one morning in December to find a detachment of soldiers boarding up the front of their home.

She immediately shrank back into the doorway of the building nearest to her on the opposite side of the street from the bakery, her heart pounding with fear for the safety of her parents. She wasn't unduly surprised when the door behind her opened slightly and she was pulled inside.

'What's happening?' she whispered frantically, her voice full of dread. 'Where are my parents? I must find out.' She made as though to open the door again. Her only thought was to find out what had happened and why.

Their neighbour wrapped her arms around her.

'They've been arrested, Florentine. It was about twenty minutes ago when the soldiers stormed in and hustled them out and the customers who were in the shop at the time. We've been looking out for you. There is a warrant out for your arrest also, and many others.'

Florentine detached herself determinedly from the comforting arms.

'I must find out where they are! Let me go, please! I must find them!'

'No! No! It will serve no purpose!'

But Florentine had already wrenched at the door once more and tumbled out into the street, straight into the arms of a man dressed in dark clothing. For a wild moment she thought it was Charles but quickly realised that it wasn't.

It was Pierre.

He firmly hustled her back into the house.

'Don't do anything to bring attention to yourself!' he warned. 'They are already out looking for you. We need to get you into hiding.'

'But Maman and Papa have been arrested! I must find them!'

'Don't you think everyone on the island feels like that? Over two hundred arrests have been made. They have pounced on every town and village at the same time.' He stroked her hair back from her face and smiled. 'Try not to worry. I don't think they'll do anything too hasty and, in the meantime, we'll get you to a place of safety.'

'I can't think of my safety! Not when my parents . . . '

'You must! It won't help them if you are arrested, too. Come, I've got a group of boys out there keeping watch at the back. Let's see if the coast is clear.' He glanced at the anxious face of their temporary hostess. 'The longer we stay here the more danger for Madame Corbe.'

Madame Corbe handed Florentine an old shawl and a padded cushion. She forced a smile.

Pierre took hold of Florentine's hand and pulled her with him. They could see a boy lounging against the far corner of the street. He made an almost imperceptible beckoning movement with his hand.

'Where are we going?' Florentine asked Pierre, as he laid his good arm protectively around her shoulders, as if helping his very pregnant wife.

'To the farm,' he replied. 'You'll be safe there. Angelique will be pleased!'

Neither of them saw Charles step out from the other end of the street. In spite of Florentine's head being covered by a shawl, Charles immediately knew who it was whom his brother, Pierre, was escorting down the street. He had caught a glimpse of her face as she turned to speak to Pierre, and the delighted smile that greeted whatever it was his brother had said to her.

His lip curled in derision. Had they no shame!

He wished he hadn't heard about her parents' arrest and that he had immediately rushed to their home to warn her, maybe to stop her before she arrived there and walked into danger.

But he hadn't moved quickly enough, it seemed. Pierre had got here before him. That surprised him. He had known how Florentine felt about Pierre, of course, but he had thought it to be a one-sided affair, one that existed entirely in Florentine's imagination.

How could they do this to Angelique? She didn't deserve to be betrayed like this. He cared little for his own heartache. It was his own fault that he had once more allowed himself to be hurt by Florentine's obsession with his brother. But Angelique was entirely innocent and unsuspecting.

He turned away, his heart cold. There were secret missions being planned, missions requiring volunteers. That was all that was left for him. Anything to relieve this unbearable pain deep within him.

He didn't look back.

Two hundred and sixty-two persons were arrested from amongst the residents of Île d'Oleron that day. Some were interned in the citadel at Le Chateau; others were released after questioning. Monsieur and Madame Devreux were among the former. Their rooftop look-out post had been denounced by persons unknown.

December saw an icy-cold spell sweep across the island. There was less food available since the mass arrests and every household felt the loss. Farmers concealed what they could from their German oppressors and managed to distribute basic requirements to the more needy. Even so, a poor Christmas was expected by all.

If Florentine had been asked what she would like for Christmas, she would have had two requests. The first would have been the release of her parents, who were still imprisoned within the citadel, so near and yet so far away.

Her second request would have been for a radio transmitter and receiver. She refused to even think of her third request, that the love she carried in her heart for Charles might somehow be requited.

Santa Claus came early that year, on December twenty-first to be exact, when the first radio set was brought to the island by Pierre Joguet. His first contact, the headmaster of the school at

Dolus, swiftly came under suspicion and the set had to be hurriedly passed on to another recipient.

A second radio set came to the isle in January, 1945, and was installed at La Chevalerie, just outside the town of Le Chateau. Florentine was overjoyed. At last she and Angela could take a share of the responsibility of signalling all the German troop movements and positions of artillery to the Allied armies on the mainland. The islands no longer felt quite so isolated.

All they needed now was a united plan of attack to overcome the German soldiers and regain possession of their island.

Florentine knew that the leaders of the Resistance were working on it. She felt so impatient! But she knew they had to be very careful about who knew their plans. They couldn't risk further betrayal.

Angela had been looking a bit peaky since Christmas but, as spring brought the island's flora to life and the scent of mimosa once more perfumed the air, Florentine was pleased to see her cheeks begin to blossom again and she wasn't too surprised when her friend confided to her in a whisper that she was expecting a baby in the autumn.

'I do hope it will be a freedom baby,' Angela sighed. 'I hate the thought of our baby being born a prisoner.'

'It will,' Florentine promised, hoping her optimism was justified. 'What does Pierre think? Is he pleased?'

'I haven't told him yet,' Angela confessed. 'I'm afraid he will try to wrap me in cotton wool and not let me beyond the boundary of the farm. After waiting all this time for the transmitters, I couldn't bear not to be part of it all!'

Florentine understood Angela's reluctance to be sidelined.

'I somehow don't think Pierre will be kept in ignorance for long though.' She smiled. 'A farmer is used to thinking in rhythms and seasons, and you look too healthy to be true!'

As soon as Pierre came home later that morning, they knew that something was in the air. His whole demeanour spoke of a pent-up excitement even as he entered the kitchen.

Angela flew into his arms, her face held up for a kiss. The smile of contentment at her friend's joy on Florentine's face froze as another figure followed Pierre into the kitchen.

It was Charles.

Florentine hadn't seen him since before Christmas but she knew he was on the island. The old heartache threatened to burst within her and she wished she could excuse herself from the family scene. She had no justifiable rights to be there, after all. No-one would miss her.

It was Pierre who stopped her as she tried to sidle past him and Angela, who was still enfolded within his one-armed embrace. If she had tried to pass on the other side, he would have been unable to stop her without making a fuss but, as it was, he merely extended the arm that held Angela close to his chest.

'Don't go, Florentine,' he said quietly. 'This is for you as well as Angela.' He smiled at Angela in adoration. 'But, before I speak, I think my darling wife has something to tell me, haven't you, angel?'

Angela blushed and cast a sidelong glance at Florentine, knowing her secret was out. She smiled in resignation, not entirely displeased to be telling him. After all, she could twist him round her little finger if she chose to. It would make no immediate difference to her war work.

'You're going to be a father,' she said, her cheeks dimpling prettily. 'Sometime around September, I should think.'

Pierre swooped her close by his good arm, a delighted grin on his face.

'I knew it, you minx! Why didn't you tell me sooner?'

'I didn't want to distract you from your work until I had to.'

Angela smiled, her heart full of love for Pierre.

'You've distracted me since the day I met you!' Pierre grinned. He turned to Charles. 'Didn't I tell you how wonderful married life is? Now I'm to be a father as well!'

'Congratulations!' Charles said, clasping his brother by his shoulders. 'And you, Angelique!'

Florentine wondered why his smile didn't quite reach his eyes. She had felt his glance upon her and had avoided looking at him until his eyes were elsewhere. Something was bothering him. She looked back at Pierre and saw something of the same light there.

Angela also became aware of some tension in the air. She pulled away a little from Pierre's embrace.

'What's the matter?' she asked.

Pierre held her away from him, so that he could look into her eyes as he spoke.

'Our plans are nearly ready,' he said quietly. 'We don't know how things will go and I want you to go back to England where you and our baby will be safe.'

The colour faded from Angela's face. 'No!' she whispered. 'I don't want to leave you! My place is here with you! *Please don't make me go!*'

Pierre gently drew his finger down the side of her face, tracing a line across to her lips before lowering his head and kissing them. 'I must,' he urged. 'You know how it's been, all the suspicions and accusations. I've got to prove my loyalty to the cause! *I'll be in the thick of it.* I want to know you are safe.'

Angela stepped back, her eyes brimming with tears. 'And I want to know you are safe, too! How do you think I'll feel, miles away across the sea? I want to be here with you.'

Pierre shook his head.

'I've made our plans. I'm taking you before the end of the week.'

He turned to face Florentine, who was feeling like an intruder as she listened to their entreaties.

'And I want you to go with us, Florentine.'

11

She wasn't totally sure that she agreed with him in saying that Angela must return to England but at least she could understand his reasoning behind it.

Angela had seized upon Pierre's words and heard only that, although she would be parted from her husband, she wouldn't be being parted from her friend.

'Oh, yes, Florentine! Do say you will! That will make it not quite so unbearable to be leaving Pierre.'

She turned to Pierre, her eyes shining with her love for him.

Florentine hated to dispel Angela's pleasure but, really, she had no choice. Her eyes were sad and she held out both of her hands towards her friend.

'I'm sorry, Angela, but it won't be possible.'

Charles spoke at the same moment. 'That's impossible, I'm afraid.'

His voice was harsher than Florentine's and carried more weight. The other three all turned towards him, various depths of puzzlement on their faces.

Charles looked thoughtful, as if he were about to reconsider his opinion. His eyes shifted from Florentine's face to Pierre's and, for once, seemed momentarily indecisive.

Florentine had a flash of comprehension. He thought she wanted to take advantage of Angela's absence to make a move on Pierre. How dare he! That was the last thing on her mind. She turned back to Pierre.

'Maybe you should take Angela, Pierre, and stay in England with her until the war is over. That would end the crazy speculation about you being the collaborator.'

'No! How could I run away like that? They would think it was because I am guilty. I will take Angelique to England but I must return as soon as I have her to safety.'

Fighting her tears, Angela nodded. 'Yes,' she whispered. 'I understand.'

Florentine faced Charles, fighting the urge to admit that it was her love for him that bound her to the island, not feelings for Pierre.

'And what of me?' she asked lightly. 'Will I be using the transmitters as liaison?'

'No. We need you out in the salines. Daniel Mann will operate the radio transmitter. You will be part of our sabotage team. There's a meeting planned between our local leaders and Captain Leclerc's lot.' He turned to Pierre. 'If you intend to take Angelique to England yourself, Pierre, and return in time to take part in the action, I suggest you do it at the earliest opportunity.'

A gleam of excitement shone in his eyes.

'It won't be long, now!'

Pierre studied the tides and, together

175

with a local fisherman who had been at school with him, he planned Angela's departure for the next moonless night.

Once the date had been settled, the days flew by. Pierre chose the departure point on the unmanned Atlantic coast, where only wooden replica weapons now stood.

Angela bade Florentine goodbye tearfully.

'You will be godmother to our baby, won't you? Maybe you and Charles?' She forced a mischievous grin on to her face.

'It will be my greatest pleasure, though I'm not too sure about Charles. Anyway, if this is all over soon, who knows, we might see each other before then.'

They hugged each other tightly and, at last, stood apart.

'Au revoir! And God be with you!'

Florentine watched until they were out of sight. At that moment, she felt as though she would never see Angela again and it tore through to her heart.

She knew that Charles stood close behind her. She could feel the warmth from his body and she longed to be able to turn into his comforting embrace and hear him whisper words of encouragement to her.

But, that was impossible and so, instead, she turned briskly about, blinking her eyes free of glistening tears.

'We'd better be getting back,' she quipped lightly.

As predicted, people took Pierre's temporary disappearance to mean that he had slipped away whilst he could, reinforcing the suspicions against him as the likely collaborator.

Extra militia and munitions were landed secretly by night and were distributed by different groups throughout the island.

Charles tried to put all thoughts of Florentine out of his head. He had too much responsibility in the coming operation to be able to waste a single second on personal matters.

Even so, he couldn't help returning

time and time again to the last time he had seen Florentine and Pierre together. There had been no sign of any subterfuge between them.

Could he have been mistaken about them?

If only the dear, darling girl wasn't so stubborn and independent. He should have swept her off her feet long ago and filled her heart and mind with love for him.

By the end of April, everything was ready. The remaining members of the Resistance who remained at liberty were divided into groups, each under a local leader who was to work in co-operation with an officer from the mainland passing on tactical expertise to add to their local knowledge.

Charles was placed with the group from La Chevalerie, whose mission was to destroy the lines of telecommunications between enemy personnel and to immobilise enemy transport.

Florentine was placed with the group who were to lead militia from the mainland through the salines to join those already on the island. The group from Boyardville was charged with preventing the destruction of the port, which had been mined by the enemy.

Pierre returned and joined the group that Charles was in. Angela was safe in England and was on her way to her parents' home. There had been delays, he explained, and he had not been allowed to travel with her.

They had little time to dwell on it. Operation Jupiter was timed to begin on April 30, at the dawn of the day.

Within six hours, all groups had completed their initial tasks of sabotage. All lines of enemy communication had been cut and the electricity cables cut, depriving the Germans of power. Over the entire island, ambushes were made, small enemy posts were attacked and a number of prisoners taken.

On May 1, Leclerc met with the group at La Cotiniere and took the battery there and at La Remigeasse. In the afternoon, the group at Boyardville took their town captive. By nightfall, the Germans had capitulated. The island was entirely in the hands of the Resistance.

Île d'Oleron was free of the yoke of Germany.

There had been small skirmishes and many groups had been split up in the fighting. Florentine hurried back to the St Clare farm. She knew the battle had been won, but at what personal cost?

No-one was there! Where were they all?

She hurried into the town, running all the way, being hailed by friends and neighbours and sharing in their jubilation, but, inside, her fears were growing. Where was Charles? Where was Pierre?

The noise of celebration rang out from the market square and from the church bells, soaring over the rooftops and along the streets. It seemed as though everyone who lived in the town was there.

She found her parents, dazed and

bewildered by their sudden release from the citadel. They hugged and wept and hugged again. Florentine hurried on. Where was Charles?

Fear began to get at her heart. There had been a few casualties. No-one knew the details yet. A number had been injured; a small handful killed.

Someone's heart would weep with sorrow this day, but did it have to be hers? So what if he no longer loved her. As long as he was alive, she could live with that.

Charles! Charles!

She didn't know if she had called aloud or not, but, suddenly, a tall figure in the midst of a crowd turned towards her. For a second, she didn't know if it were Charles or Pierre and she halted in front of him, her eyes searching anxiously through the grime on his face.

She didn't know how she knew, but she did.

'Charles!'

Her heart leaped within her as she

spoke his name and she started forward.

Charles held out his arms and she ran into them, sobbing into his chest, 'You're safe! You're safe!'

Oh, it felt so good! She nestled into him, her arms around his waist, her head against his chest feeling his heartbeat, wrapped in his love.

Or was she?

She drew herself away slowly and looked at him. Her breath caught in her throat. His expression was one of uncertainty. She was embarrassing him.

'I'm sorry, Charles,' she mumbled. 'I'm glad you're all right. I . . . I . . . '

She couldn't say any more. She would disgrace herself with more tears if she tried to say anymore. She turned away, her face burning with shame and disappointment.

'Florentine! Wait! There's something I must say!'

No! He was going to say she'd left it too late! And could she blame him? She simply hadn't known her own heart until she had met him again . . . and even then she had stubbornly fought him every step of the way.

Charles strode after Florentine and seized hold of her by her shoulders.

'Will you stand still and listen to me for once in your life!' he shouted at her. 'You really are the most exasperating woman I have ever had any dealing with!'

Florentine felt a spark of hope flicker within her.

She looked at him silently.

His hair was unkempt, his clothes looked as though they were fit only for the fire, his face was streaked with black oil and his red-rimmed eyes betrayed the fact that he had had no sleep for three days. He looked like an escaped criminal.

'Have you had many dealings with women then?' she asked coolly, raising her eyebrow.

She suddenly knew just where his anger was coming from, but she didn't intend to make it easy for him! Not after the heartache he had given her since her return to the island . . . was it still less than a year ago?

'No! Not many!'

His voice had lost much of its fury, and his expression was almost benign. 'Hardly any,' he amended lamely. 'In fact . . . '

He grasped hold of her shoulders and made her face him squarely.

' . . . there's only ever been one woman who has made any impression on me. And she's the most exasperating woman you could ever hope to meet.'

Florentine's heart leaped with hope.

'Really? And this woman, the only one who has ever made an impression on you, have you ever told her what she means to you?'

Charles's hands moved from her shoulders to cup around her face.

'Not recently. She never stands still long enough for me to put my thoughts in order,' he said softly, his lips beginning to twitch into the vestiges of a smile.

'Then, maybe, you should practise right here and now. We could pretend I'm not here and you could close your eyes and say whatever it is you would like to say to her. It won't go any further.'

Charles smiled.

'She's incorrigible, endearing, vexing and delightful. She's adorable, infuriating, exasperating and enchanting. She argues until I'm fractious and yet has only to flash her eyes at me to make me burn like a ball of fire deep within. It's like being engulfed by an incurable disease and knowing there will be no respite from it this side of eternity. Have you any suggestions as to how I might capture this exquisite creature and make her my own?'

They were grinning idiotically at each other.

Florentine's heart was racing. She could feel the warmth of his breath upon her lips and she raised herself up on to her toes to be nearer to him. She felt giddy with expectation and fearful of not receiving his kisses.

And she couldn't bear to wait another second!

'I think,' she said quietly, 'that you should kiss her right now and leave all the talking until later. You might find that she's already yours . . . and always has been, although she didn't realise it!'

THE END